Viral Vengeance

A Medical Thriller

By Norma Rose

For my husband.

Your encouragement and constant support made this book a reality.

Acknowledgement

Many thanks to all my family and friends who supported me throughout this process.

A special note of gratitude to Betsy, Paul, and Jacki for taking time to analyze and provide feedback on my first manuscript.

Table of Contents

Prologue xi
Chapter One 1
Chapter Two 18
Chapter Three 42
Chapter Four 52
Chapter Five 62
Chapter Six 75
Chapter Seven 82
Chapter Eight 87
Chapter Nine 93
Chapter Ten 99
Chapter Eleven 104
Chapter Twelve 119
Chapter Thirteen 125
Chapter Fourteen 138
Chapter Fifteen 146
Chapter Sixteen 152
Chapter Seventeen 155
Chapter Eighteen 162
Chapter Nineteen 169
Chapter Twenty 174
Chapter Twenty-One 182
Chapter Twenty-Two 187
Chapter Twenty-Three 190
Chapter Twenty-Four 198
Chapter Twenty-Five 202
Chapter Twenty-Six 211
Chapter Twenty-Seven 217
Chapter Twenty-Eight 228
Chapter Twenty-Nine 233
Chapter Thirty 240
Chapter Thirty-one 246
Chapter Thirty-Two 251
Afterword 254

x

Prologue

The scalpel flashed under the OR lights as Dr. Mariah Gordon began a surgery that might take her patient's life and change hers forever. The situation demanded lightning-fast technique. She incised the skin stretched tightly over the womb; the rest was done bluntly to minimize bleeding. Using only her fingers, she pulled the muscles apart and opened the womb; the baby and placenta were delivered in less than a minute.

Blood poured from the womb, filling the open abdomen and spilling onto the floor. Suction could not keep the surgical field clear of blood. Dr. Gordon pulled the womb up onto the abdomen, above the flow of blood, and swiftly sutured.

"Sew like the wind!" Dr. Haji, her medical school mentor, would say when the bleeding was heavy. Her patient was dying. Ten units of blood—more than all the blood in a woman's body—and just as many units of clotting factors were infusing as fast as the IV tubing would allow. Removing the placenta cured the cause of the bleeding, but that did not mean the patient would survive.

Twelve hours prior...

Chapter One

Captain Mariah Gordon, MD, threw her briefcase and overnight bag into the back of her car and looked up at her apartment building, catching a glimpse of Emery, her boyfriend, standing at the kitchen window. Jet contrails glowed blood red and caught her attention as they slashed across the dawn sky. Mariah's glance returned to the kitchen window, hoping Emery noticed the dramatic sunrise; he was gone. The memory of his warm embrace lifted her spirits as she faced another long day at the hospital.

Mariah glanced at her watch: 6:30 a.m. She balanced her travel mug of coffee on the console as she backed her old Ford Maverick, affectionately called "Irving," out of the parking space. The car reminded Mariah of her grandfather who scoffed at modern luxuries, was often malodorous, and was her most faithful childhood friend. Irving didn't have modern conveniences like electric windows or a cup holder, and the smell of burning oil from his exhaust was especially strong this morning.

Once on the highway, Mariah checked her hair in the rearview mirror, ensuring it was all tucked up in military fashion. It was thick and curly, and she liked how it looked off duty. But Mariah was a fourth-year OB-GYN resident at Brewster Army Medical Center and a captain in the US Army; at work, her hair was tamed into an old-fashioned bun.

The thirty-minute commute allowed Mariah time to mentally review the day ahead. She was on call tonight and scheduled to work all day tomorrow. She wondered what this day would bring; a lot could happen in a day and a half.

Did I forget my overnight bag? A quick glance over her shoulder reminded her it was in the backseat. *Calm down*, she thought to herself. *It's just another night on call.*

Mariah turned her thoughts to Emery. He was her first serious boyfriend. A young lawyer in a prestigious law firm in Philadelphia, he was blond, athletic, and very handsome. They met in Philadelphia five years ago. Mariah was riding the bus to the University of Pennsylvania campus when a tire blew out. To avoid being late for class, she tried to hail a taxi in front of the broken-down bus during rush hour traffic. Mariah stood in the right lane of Walnut Street, blocking the entrance to a parking lot, and waved her hand as a taxi drove past. Emery Davison, a law student at the university, was driving behind the taxi. He planned to park in the lot next to the bus and almost ran Mariah over as she stood in his lane. He pulled alongside and rolled down his window, planning to shout something profane. Mariah's green eyes, outlined by dark lashes, looked at him from a pale, perfectly oval face framed by dark curly hair blown everywhere by the wind. Emery was caught off guard by her striking beauty. He offered her a ride, and their conversation kindled a friendship that quickly evolved into a serious love affair.

A final swig of cold coffee reminded Mariah that she was almost there. Wedging the empty mug between the seat and the gearshift, she pulled into the staff parking lot for Brewster Army Medical Center (BAMC). It was Thursday morning, May 27, 1999, in San Antonio, Texas; the sun was slicing through the buildings, preheating the parking lot like an oven. Memories of last evening and of enjoying coffee in bed with Emery vanished as she turned Irving off and waited for him to cough and gasp into silence. She rechecked her hair and then grabbed her briefcase and overnight bag from the backseat.

BAMC was one of the US Army's oldest hospitals and medical training centers; the original hospital building was in the National Registry of Historic Places. Several wings of the building were remodeled, giving the hospital an incongruous feeling of history spliced with modern technology. Mariah entered the hospital through a side door and waited for the staff elevator; the basement lobby smelled familiar, like a library, not acrid or biological like other hospitals. The staff elevator was small, with decorative mirrors on three walls framed with gold molding, left over from bygone days when hospitals were more formal and less sterile.

The elevator doors parted on the first floor.

"Good morning!" Mariah greeted two residents as they punched the fifth-floor button. "A surgeon *and* an anesthesiologist going to labor and delivery together? I don't know what's happening upstairs, but it can't be good!"

"Hi, Mariah," Mark Stewart replied. "We both worked all night and just sat down to breakfast when our pagers went off. What's going on up there?" Mark was a fourth-year general surgery resident. He was wearing a white lab coat over his faded blue scrubs.

"I'm just coming in and haven't heard a thing." Mariah pulled her beeper out of her pocket and checked that it was on and charged. She had not been paged.

"Why doesn't the OB chief resident know what's going on before *we're* called up there to help out?" whined Andy Daniels, an anesthesia resident.

The elevator doors opened on the fifth floor; the two residents stepped aside, allowing Mariah to exit first. She walked straight across the hall to the C-section operating room. There was a patient on the OR table being prepped for C-section. Her swollen, pregnant belly was scrubbed and painted orange with an iodine solution called Betadine—the belly looked like a basketball protruding from the blue OR sheets. Mariah nodded across the OR to the OB-GYN resident on call to let him know she was there and able to help if needed. She glanced at the clock on the wall: 0710 military hours.

Next, Mariah turned to the delivery room across the hall and saw the problem. A second-year OB-GYN resident was trying to control a postpartum hemorrhage after a vaginal delivery. It was obvious that there had been a lot of blood loss; the patient was in the Trendelenburg position. The delivery table was tilted backward, placing

—
4

the patient's hips higher than her head. This was a fast and easy way to maintain circulation to the patient's brain during rapid blood loss.

"What can I do?" Mariah asked as she put on a surgical mask and entered the delivery room.

Grabbing a sterile gown and booties, she began covering her uniform with protective, blue paper garments. The patient moaned as the resident vigorously massaged her uterus, trying to get it to contract and stop bleeding.

The resident gasped, "Need help managing the bleeding. Uterus is boggy; I can't get it to firm up."

Mariah understood. The uterus is an amazing organ that nourishes and protects the baby, but if it doesn't contract after delivery, the bleeding can be lethal.

Mariah shot a look across the room at Mark and Andy standing uncomfortably in the doorway of the delivery room. "Mark, see if they need you to assist in the C-section. Andy, come here. Help us with this patient. She needs a second IV and fluids running wide open."

Mariah turned to the resident. "What have you done so far? Have you checked for a retained placenta? How much Pitocin have you given her?"

After a few minutes, the uterus began to contract, and the bleeding slowed. Blood was ready in the blood bank for transfusion, but the patient's vital signs had stabilized. Mariah decided to watch her closely with serial blood counts and not transfuse blood at this time.

Once the situation was under control, the patient's husband picked up their crying newborn and placed her in his wife's arms. The fear and confusion of postpartum hemorrhage faded as she soothed her baby and calmly began breastfeeding.

Mariah carefully removed her blood-soaked surgical gown, gloves, and booties and looked at the clock: 0845 hours. No time for patient rounds. A quick check in at the OB floor's nursing station before Morning Report Conference would have to suffice.

Click, click. Mariah's black heels sounded out against the tiled hallway in sharp contrast to the quiet rubber-soled shoes the nurses wore. Her army uniform fit well, and the heels gave an impressive look to an otherwise dowdy green skirt and blouse. The army required all doctors to wear a uniform in the hospital unless actively performing surgery or managing labor patients. Mariah wished she could work in scrubs all day like her fellow civilian residents in nonmilitary residency programs.

Major Karen Blythe, head nurse for the OB floor, stood at the nurses' station taking notes on her clipboard. She was responsible for everything that occurred on the OB floor. High-risk pregnant patients, both local and from surrounding military community hospitals in Texas and other nearby states, were sent to BAMC for specialized obstetric care. These pregnant women were like ticking time bombs developing into an emergency at any moment, and Karen's nurses were not going to be caught off guard. Each patient was evaluated daily with fetal heart rate monitoring and ultrasound. Mariah learned long ago that if she wanted accurate, up-to-date information about the OB inpatients, she had to talk to Karen.

"How did the delivery go?" Karen asked.

"OK. The postpartum hemorrhage was a problem at first, but the patient is fine now. I don't think she'll need a blood transfusion. We need to watch her closely with serial blood counts and try to track her urine output...but you already knew that!" Mariah smiled. "How are the patients on the floor?"

Karen looked down at the notes on her clipboard. "Everyone was quiet last night. The preterm labor patient in room 512 developed some contractions and went over to labor and delivery for monitoring. She received some IV fluids, did not progress into labor, and returned to the ward around midnight."

"Good! How's O'Rielly's blood pressure today?"

"One hundred thirty-eight over ninety, which is really good considering it was taken after she yelled at the nurse for waking her up."

Mariah knew Megan O'Rielly was a problem for the nurses. Megan was a sixteen-year-old with severe preeclampsia. This was a serious condition: it caused high blood pressure and potentially dangerous organ damage for the mother. There could be blood flow problems for the fetus. The only cure was delivery, and Megan's pregnancy was too premature to deliver now, so she remained in the hospital under close observation until delivery. Being sixteen and admitted to the hospital for weeks of bed rest, blood tests, and fetal monitoring was difficult, and Megan made everyone aware of her suffering.

Karen pointed over Mariah's shoulder. "Looks like your team is ready for rounds!"

Mariah turned to greet the two doctors on her OB team. "Good morning, team!" Mariah smiled; she enjoyed teaching residents.

The intern and second-year OB-GYN residents were on call last night. Both held a large cup of coffee and desperately needed a shower. Mariah smiled encouragingly; she knew how hard it was to get started in the morning after working all night. "It's late. Let's go straight to the conference room. You can tell me the highlights of your OB patients along the way."

As a medical student, Mariah had nervous energy that fueled her enthusiasm for working all night during her OB clinical rotation. She admired the OB-GYN residents' ability to treat pregnant patients with complicated medical illnesses, and felt that delivering babies at all hours of the night was thrilling. Mariah chose OB-GYN because the lifestyle and surgery challenged her physically, and the medical management of obstetric and gynecologic patients challenged her intellectually. She hoped the gratification of doing a job she loved could outweigh the burden of long hours at the hospital.

When Mariah began her internship, her mother commented, "Doing surgery and caring for patients after working twenty-four hours doesn't seem wise to me. How can you learn anything when you're that tired?"

Mariah knew her mother had a point, but there

was no alternative, and she wasn't going to give up her career just because it was hard work. OB-GYN residencies lasted four years, and Mariah put her life on "hold" to ensure she completed her training successfully.

Her boyfriend, Emery, understood her sacrifice and made few demands of her. He lived and worked as a lawyer in Philadelphia and visited her as often as possible. Together, they looked forward to Mariah's graduation from residency and the beginning of a more normal relationship.

Mariah's team finished their review of the OB inpatients as they climbed the stairs to the sixth floor. BAMC's OB-GYN residency program had sixteen residents, four in each year of residency. Every doctor in the OB-GYN department was required to attend Morning Report. The small conference room overflowed with interns, residents, and attending doctors seated in a semicircle and facing a small, wooden podium. Attending doctors were the principal instructors of the residency, and they sat in the front row along with the fourth-year residents, also known as "chiefs." The rest of the residents filled in the second and third rows; interns and medical students stood against the back wall.

The chief resident on call reviewed any critical or interesting cases, as well as all unscheduled OR cases from the past twenty-four hours. Once this discussion concluded, the GYN chief resident took over the podium and asked for any other important patient cases to be discussed, reviewed a fundamental learning point, and dismissed the residents to start the workday.

Mariah sat next to Dr. Jenna Blackstone, her best friend in the residency program. Jenna's energy and enthusiasm inspired Mariah. She had short, strawberry-blond hair, and she loved practical jokes and her husband, Floyd. She had transferred to BAMC three years ago and filled a vacant resident position in Mariah's second year of residency. They quickly became friends and occasionally carpooled to work.

Dr. Sam Michaels stood at the podium, looking tired and unshaven, still wearing his bloody scrubs. "Last night there were two vaginal deliveries and one C-section. All went smoothly." A native Texan, Sam spoke slowly and deliberately. His southwestern drawl conveyed a calm manner that put patients at ease, and Sam never seemed to let anything get under his skin.

Mariah envied his down-to-earth character; too bad his wife didn't find it appealing. There was a rumor that Sam's wife threatened him with divorce; she was tired of being left alone while he worked long hours at the hospital. He never mentioned family troubles at work.

Sam discussed the simultaneous C-section and vaginal delivery, complicated by postpartum hemorrhage. He began with the routine description of a pregnant patient:

"A twenty-six-year-old white female, Gravida five, Para four, presented to labor and delivery in active labor at five centimeters dilation with a breech baby."

Mariah remembered the first time she heard the

words "Gravida" and "Para" during her OB rotation in medical school. An intern presented a patient who was pregnant with twins and confused the terms. The senior resident explained that "Gravida" referred to the number of pregnancies a woman had experienced, and "Para" referred to the number of deliveries a woman had experienced.

Sam continued, "Ultrasound done at the bedside showed a nine-pound baby in breech position, and the decision was made to perform a C-section."

Sam's voice was soft, and Mariah had to strain to hear him. "The patient's labor was progressing fast. At the same time, a twenty-one-year-old female, whose labor was being induced for low amniotic fluid levels, was also fully dilated. Since the two patients were going to deliver at the same time, I decided to perform the C-section with my intern and informed Dr. Patterson that he would be on his own in the delivery room. He delivered a healthy, six-pound, six-ounce baby girl complicated by a postpartum hemorrhage. He paged the anesthesia and surgery chief residents for help since I was scrubbed in with the C-section and Dr. Nelson was at home."

Even though anesthesia and surgical residents were not trained in obstetrics, their expertise in blood loss was helpful when the OB doctor was shorthanded.

"Always remember, if you are going down, take as many specialties with you as you can," Dr. David Mettson joked softly to Mariah.

Dr. Mettson was a gynecologic oncologist and had

lots of surgical experience. He had a friendly, healthy happiness about him that Mariah appreciated. Last year when his wife announced she was pregnant, David asked Mariah to be her private doctor. Three months ago, Mariah delivered his son, Jared. He always had time and good advice for her, no matter the problem, and he was a cool surgeon in the face of catastrophe.

Mariah admired David; he was a great doctor, father, and husband. He seemed to have everything that she wanted. With a good career, excellent training, and a boyfriend like Emery, she believed she was guaranteed happiness, just like David.

"Also, around midnight," Sam added, "a GYN patient was admitted due to worsening pain and fever after a miscarriage. I started antibiotics and did a D and C in the procedure room. The patient is doing much better this morning."

He picked up his note sheet and started to leave the podium when Dr. Halligan, the grizzled chief of gynecology, cleared his throat, and the conference took a turn from congenial to confrontational.

Dr. Halligan had twenty years of experience at Dallas's Parkland Hospital in the days before *Roe v. Wade*. His memories were forever tainted by images of wards filled with women who lay infected and sometimes dying after undergoing illegal, backroom abortions. His mission was to ensure that every resident understood how quickly a young, healthy woman with an infection in her womb could get sick and die.

Agitated by Sam's D and C case, he asked, "What was her pulse when you admitted her?"

Sam responded, "Ninety-five."

Halligan hurled, "What was her blood pressure?"

Sam calmly replied, "Ninety over forty."

In a healthy young woman, Mariah thought to herself, *these vital signs are normal, but in a patient with an infection, they can indicate the patient is getting sicker and might be developing sepsis.*

Dr. Halligan was working himself into a tirade.

"Why the hell did you choose to do the D and C in the procedure room instead of the OR? Once her blood pressure drops, she'll be extremely difficult to resuscitate, especially in that damn closet of a procedure room. Do you know what happens if her BP drops, and you can't get it back up?"

Dr. Halligan stopped for a moment and looked around the room to ensure every resident was paying attention as he answered his own question. "She's gonna DIE!"

This was not the first time they had heard Dr. Halligan's rant about managing a young, healthy patient with an infection in her uterus, and it usually ended with a reference to death.

Sam had to justify his decision to use the small procedure room on the sixth floor, where he was alone and responsible for everything: patient sedation, pain control, and the procedure; usually he was teaching the techniques to a junior resident on call with him. That procedure room was nicknamed the "Closet." Mariah shivered slightly, remembering her experience in the Closet with a patient becoming unresponsive during a D and C last fall. Sedation combined with pain medication can cause a patient to stop breathing. It was such a harrowing experience that she vowed to never do another procedure in the Closet again.

Mariah silently reaffirmed her own mantra: "Never sacrifice patient safety by taking shortcuts." This was Mariah's last rotation of her four-year residency; she was graduating in six weeks. Her next assignment was at Mitchell Army Community Hospital in Georgia. This meant she would be at a small hospital with no specialists to help with critical cases. Mariah was determined to absorb every practical application of patient care she could before she began that duty.

The conclusion of Sam's report brought no comment from the row of attending doctors. This was interpreted as, "Good job, Sam."

Kirsten Smith, the GYN chief resident who chaired Morning Report, looked at her watch. She announced, "We seem to have gone overtime. You're all dismissed unless anyone has anything important to share." No one spoke as they got up and exited the conference room, anxious to escape the stifling atmosphere of Morning Report.

"Only twenty-four more to go," Mariah said to herself. Tomorrow morning would be her turn at the podium.

Checking her watch, she thought: *OB clinic begins in ten minutes. Still not enough time to see the OB inpatients—I'll have to make rounds during lunch break.*

Instead, Mariah went to the residents' office. This "office" was a large room located at the far end of the GYN ward. It was filled with old, discarded desks, some chairs, and a few shelves arranged against the walls. Each chief resident had a large desk with medical charts strewn, tossed, or piled neatly over the work surface. Second- and third-year residents shared desks depending on which service they were working: GYN, GYN ONC, OB, or RE. Interns rotated every month and did not sign off on charts, so they were not assigned a desk. If they needed a workspace, they could use an old, broken cart that was pushed into the far corner.

As Mariah entered, she found herself in the middle of an audience watching Kirsten Smith show off her latest jazz class dance steps. Kirsten was a mother of two adolescent daughters, and her "ne'er do well" husband was either thrilling her by helping out with the kids, or threatening to leave her. Mariah never could keep track. Maybe as a release from all the stress at work and home, Kirsten went overboard doing feminine projects. She knit during Morning Report, baked cakes and cookies, and took dance lessons with her kids.

Today, she was demonstrating her latest dance moves on top of her desk, ending with a high kick just as Dr. Halligan walked in. Dr. Halligan rarely entered the residents' office. When he did, he usually paused in the doorway, barked orders to the GYN chief resident, and then retreated to his private office where he smoked cigarettes and read journals. It was common knowledge that he never spoke to any resident on his team except the GYN chief resident; it was the chief's job to disseminate Dr. Halligan's wisdom to the junior residents.

Dr. Halligan came in the door just as Kirsten was doing her jazzy high kick, revealing navy-blue gym shorts under her green army skirt. He looked up at her and his usual stony expression began to melt into a hint of a smile.

"Kirsten, when you're done," he suggested, "can you meet me in my office to talk about that surgical patient you want me to help you with?" Shaking his head and turning to leave, he muttered, "Kids…"

Everyone burst out laughing. Kirsten jumped off the desk, smoothing her skirt and acting like she was worried she might be in trouble. The truth was, once residents made it to the last year of residency, Dr. Halligan had a lot of respect for them. As long as they worked hard, he supported them whether in surgery or at Morning Report. Unless, of course, they chose to do something dumb…like a D and C in the Closet.

Mariah looked at her desk, two large piles of charts needed signatures. She peeled off the top five charts form one stack, and quickly glanced through them. In addition to signing off verbal orders, she checked pathology and lab reports. It was a small dent in a large pile, but it made her feel productive in an otherwise unproductive morning. Then she put on her long white lab coat and clicked her black high heels back down the tiled hallway to catch the elevator to the OB clinic.

Chapter Two

As OB chief resident, Mariah was responsible for all pregnant patients in the hospital, clinic, and ER. The army provided obstetric care to all active duty females, dependent wives, and dependent daughters. A regional army medical center, BAMC accepted high-risk OB patient referrals from army community hospitals in Texas and neighboring states. Mariah's job was to work with the maternal fetal medicine specialist and ensure that every pregnant patient admitted to BAMC received excellent obstetric care.

The OB-GYN clinic was located on the first floor at the far end of the wing, past the outpatient pharmacy. Mariah picked her way through the crowd of people waiting for prescriptions. To get to the OB clinic, she had to walk through the GYN walk-in clinic waiting room. The GYN walk-in clinic provided female patients with acute GYN problems an opportunity to be seen the same day, instead of waiting weeks for an appointment or trying their luck in the ER. A single second-year OB-GYN resident staffed the walk-in clinic, and when it was busy, the patient wait time could be as long as two hours. Today was busy.

Jenna Blackstone was helping out, seeing a few walk-in patients before her GYN ONC clinic began. She caught Mariah's eye as she walked through the waiting area, and waved her over.

"You're never going to believe what I just saw!" She pulled Mariah into an empty exam room. "There's a private in room five who had a combination lock stuck in her vagina!"

Jenna had a quick wit, and she was always looking to play a practical joke. Last month, she kidnapped Mariah's high heels from her locker and left a ransom note demanding six Hershey chocolate bars if she ever wanted to see them again. Mariah started to worry she was going to be the butt of another joke.

"Says she doesn't know how it got there, and she's sticking to her story. I tried to get her to fess up, but she wouldn't talk." Jenna grinned and leaned against the empty desk, writing her office visit note in the private's chart.

"Did you get it out?" Mariah relaxed a little since there seemed to be no practical joke associated with this poor private's predicament.

"It was easy. I just grabbed it with ring forceps. Boy was she happy. I'm just going to let her go back to her company. What do you think?" Jenna smiled.

Mariah shrugged. "Seems OK to me. I just hope she's not being sexually abused in her barracks or anything. I mean, what can you do with a story like that? Call the MPs? Which is worse, letting her go without an investigation or getting her commanding officer involved?" Mariah was careful not to break a rule or fail to comply with regulations, especially where a doctor's "duty to notify" applies.

"Definitely not going to call the MPs or get her CO involved. I told her she could leave once she was dressed." Jenna rolled her eyes at the thought, but her smile never faded. "I have to go. Oncology clinic is full today, and I know there's at least one admission waiting for me."

"Never a dull moment in the walk-in clinic." Mariah said as she followed Jenna out of the exam room and through the crowded waiting area to her office.

Her morning clinic roster listed twenty names of high-risk OB patients. The top three names were already crossed off, meaning the patients were waiting for her in exam rooms. This was Mariah's typical morning schedule; she had two and a half hours to see all her patients—less than ten minutes per patient.

Mariah took the first chart out of the rack and quickly reviewed the face sheet. One careful glance at this page could tell her everything she needed to know about this patient and her pregnancy: the patient was thirty years old, pregnant with fraternal twins, and just beginning her third trimester. Her prior two deliveries were uncomplicated. Today her vital signs, lab values, and weight gain were normal.

"Hello, Mrs. Morgan." Mariah smiled at the woman sitting on the exam table, her swollen abdomen making it uncomfortable for her to sit without leaning back slightly.

Mariah's smile remained fixed as she watched Mrs. Morgan's two small children playing in the cabinets under the sink. "Hi, guys." She tried to act happy to see them again.

Mrs. Morgan needed a cervical exam, blood tests, weekly monitoring, and counseling about preterm labor. The kids interrupted Mariah on and off throughout the appointment, demanding attention.

Leaving the exam room, Mariah thought about how hard it would be to care for newborn twins and two small children.

The next patient was Penny Reynolds, an unmarried, twenty-one-year-old active duty specialist who worked in the motor pool. Penny was healthy, and her pregnancy was not high risk, but Mariah saw her in this clinic because she was her "private" patient. This meant Mariah was Penny's primary OB doctor and would attend her delivery instead of the OB resident on call. Mariah accepted Penny as a private patient as a favor for Laura Reynolds, a nurse practitioner in the family practice department.

As Mariah lifted Penny's chart out of the rack, her medical assistant came over to her and whispered, "I don't understand how two sisters can be so different. Penny is so nice and Laura is always evil to me."

"Evil seems like a harsh word; what did she do today?" Mariah whispered back. She knew Laura had a difficult personality, but she still tried to get along with her because she was an old friend of Emery's. They had gone to the same high school together and even dated for a while, though never seriously. Mariah would never have known Laura if Emery hadn't run into her at his high school reunion four years ago and discovered she was stationed at BAMC too.

Her medical assistant continued, "I hate the way she stares at me when I take Penny's weight and blood pressure, like I'm incompetent or something. She's creepy too. The medical assistants at the Family Practice Clinic hate working with her because she has no empathy for her patients. It's like she enjoys watching sick people suffer. There's something about her that's not right."

"I won't disagree with you, but Penny's my private patient, and we have to make the best of it." Mariah quickly reviewed the chart and entered the exam room.

Penny smiled and greeted Mariah eagerly. She was twenty-four weeks pregnant, just starting to show, and very excited about her pregnancy. She wanted to hear the baby's heartbeat, record it, and play it over the telephone for her mother. As the baby's heartbeat was recording, Penny blurted out for the recorder, "Her name is going to be Amanda, Mom. I'm naming her after you."

Laura, on the other hand, sat in the corner with a cold, calculated expression and observed the visit. She barely smiled when the heartbeat sounded strong and didn't join in with Penny for the recording. Her devotion to Penny was obvious, but her lack of affection made Mariah wonder why she cared so much about her sister's pregnancy.

Penny's vital signs and lab tests were normal, and

Baby Amanda sounded great on the recording. Since that happy visit took only five minutes, Mariah left the room hopeful she might catch up and finish her morning clinic on time.

The next patient was Bonnie Thompson. She was high risk because she'd had two children by C-section prior to this pregnancy, and she wanted to deliver vaginally. To make matters worse, her husband had died three months ago in a plane crash. She moved to Texas to live with her in-laws for support during her final months of pregnancy. Her son and daughter had been in the plane when it went down, and survived. Bonnie had told Mariah several times that her husband saved the kids by packing diapers and blankets around them before impact. Mariah, unsure how crucial the padding was to their survival, always became emotional at the thought of his devotion.

Seven-year-old Kyle had sustained closed head trauma and was being treated at a pediatric neurologic center in San Antonio. Four-year-old Kaylie suffered multiple broken bones. Today, she was reading a book with her mom, sitting on the exam table with her left leg and arm still in casts.

Bonnie was holding up as best she could, and her pregnancy was mercifully uncomplicated. The only problem she faced was her delivery. Bonnie controlled her grief until she thought about delivering this child without her husband. Then the depths of her loss became apparent.

"I'm not sure I can go through labor and delivery without Tom. But having an operation without him would be harder." Bonnie cried quietly into a Kleenex and gave Kaylie a tight hug.

Mariah gently encouraged her to decide soon; she was within two weeks of her due date, and her labor could start any time.

Mariah checked her watch after saying good-bye to her last patient of the morning. It was 1:00 p.m. already, and she still had rounds upstairs before starting the afternoon clinic. "No lunch today." She sighed and hit the "UP" button for the elevator.

Karen Blythe met Mariah at the nurses' station. "I knew you would make it up here to see your patients sooner or later. Did you get lunch yet?"

"No time. Hand me the vital signs clipboard. I'll try to make lightning rounds and get back to clinic before two."

Karen handed the clipboard to Mariah and said, "I wish every resident was as conscientious as you. Here you go. And I must warn you: Megan O'Rielly is on the warpath. She wants to go home and says she will sign out against medical advice."

"Oh great. I'll save her for last. Thanks for the warning. Anyone else having issues?" Mariah picked up the clipboard and a chart, and walked toward the first antepartum patient room.

"Not that I know of." Karen leaned over to the clerk at the nurses' station and asked, "Can you please call dietary and have them send up a PB and J, glass of milk, and an apple? Tell them it's for Dr. Gordon."

At 2:30 p.m., Mariah's beeper went off, and the ER's extension blinked on its display. Mariah was just getting back to clinic an hour late, and five patients were waiting for her. She picked up the phone and dialed the ER. The clerk in the ER took a few minutes to find the doctor who had paged her, and Mariah was just about to hang up the phone.

"Hi, Mariah, this is Tim Anthony, and I have two OB patients down here that I want to tell you about." That was a polite way of saying he had one, maybe two patient admissions coming her way. "The first one is an eighteen-year-old gal who is eight weeks pregnant and very dehydrated. She has been in twice with severe nausea and vomiting. We gave her IV fluids and nausea medication, but she still can't keep anything down. She needs to be admitted for more intensive hydration and therapy."

"OK, send her up to the OB floor, and I'll call orders in later." Mariah was impatient; her clinic was getting backed up. "What else have you got?"

"The second patient is a twenty-one-year-old active duty girl, Gravida one, Para zero, at twenty-four weeks, whose car was sideswiped on the highway. She looks fine but has a pretty big gash in her left thigh. Her vitals are stable, and the baby sounds good, but I want the orthopedic resident to look at that gash on her leg. She might need some stitches."

"Fine, her baby is very preterm, not quite viable, really. Call me after the orthopedics resident sees the patient, and we'll send her up to labor and delivery for observation." Mariah hung up and felt relieved she could continue to see her clinic patients for now.

The next time Mariah looked at the clock, it was 4:30 p.m.—two hours since the ER had paged her. Mariah had called the orders for IV hydration to the nurses on the OB ward two hours ago, and Karen Blythe had already informed her the patient was much improved.

Tim never called back about the patient in the motor vehicle accident with the gash on her leg. Annoyed at having to check back herself, Mariah picked up the phone and punched the ER numbers. Her clinic was almost finished, and she wanted to know what was going on with this patient.

After another brief hold, Tim came to the phone, assuring Mariah that it was "crazy busy" down in the ER that day. "Yeah, the orthopedics resident came and saw her, and felt the gash needed to be treated in the operating room. She's next in line for the OR."

"Really?" Mariah was astonished. "When were they going to tell me? Ortho can't take an OB patient to the OR without at least consulting me!" She stood up at her desk. "When is she going to the OR? Do I have time to come down and see her first? How are her vital signs and fetal heart tones?"

"The fetal heart rate is running around one hundred twenty beats per minute...I think I hear them calling for her now. Do you want to talk to the orthopedics resident right now?"

"Yes. Who is it? Have them page me. I'm still in

the OB clinic." Mariah looked at her watch.

"OK, I think Taylor's on call for orthopedics. He's been in the OR all afternoon with the driver of the other car. He only broke out briefly to see your patient. I'll have him call you." Dr. Anthony hung up.

Mariah went back to seeing her clinic patients, slightly unnerved about the whole thing. *No reason to worry*, she thought. Mariah convinced herself there was nothing more to do and waited for Taylor to call.

The last two patients in the clinic were waiting in exam rooms, and Mariah was hungry. She regretted not eating the peanut-butter-and-jelly sandwich that Karen ordered, but it had arrived after she had finished rounds. Now there was a small window of time to buy dinner from the dining hall before it closed for the night. If she didn't get there soon, "wall food," the night staff's nickname for snacks from the vending machines, would be her only dinner.

Ana Gonzalez was a thirty-eight-year-old mother of six, with poorly controlled gestational diabetes, who came to the clinic every week. Each visit, Mariah would review Ana's blood sugars and counsel her about following her diet more closely. Ideally, Ana should be started on insulin to better treat her diabetes and help prevent her baby from developing complications, but Ana refused. She had an irrational fear that she would contract diabetes for the rest of her life if she began insulin injections. Mariah tried again to explain the facts, but Ana started to cry, and Mariah decided that she would drop the subject for now.

It was 5:30 p.m. The clinic waiting room was dark and empty. Jenna had seen the last patient for Mariah half an hour ago, and there was still no word from Taylor in the ER. Three hours had elapsed since the ER first paged her, and Mariah felt unsettled. Unsure if she should go straight to the ER, Mariah called labor and delivery to see what was going on up there.

Tracy, a skillful labor and delivery nurse, answered the phone. "Labor and delivery, this is Tracy." Mariah felt reassured knowing she was on duty.

"Hi, Tracy. It's Mariah. What's going on up there?"

Mariah always used her first name when identifying herself to the nurses, though they always called her "Dr. Gordon." She felt it was unequal; she addressed them by their first names, and they called her "Doctor." Most nurses seemed to take this in stride and appreciated her congeniality.

Tracy replied, "Hi Dr. Gordon. It's pretty quiet right now." Experienced labor and delivery nurses always provided a simplified version of reality. Her reply could mean anything from an uncomplicated, solitary labor patient to multiple patients in various stages of labor and/or delivering.

Then she added, "The ER called a minute ago. They're sending up a twenty-four weeker injured in an MVA."

Mariah was relieved. "Finally. I've been waiting

for her to get to labor and delivery all afternoon." She pressed Tracy for more information. "Did they say how her surgery went? She has a gash on her leg, and orthopedics took her to the OR to treat it."

Tracy replied, "She didn't go to the OR. I guess they changed their mind and bandaged it in the ER."

Surprised she never heard from Taylor, Mariah decided the patient's condition must have been exaggerated. She had time for dinner. "I'm on my way up to labor and delivery now, but I think I'll just stop by the dining hall on the way and get a dinner tray to go. Call me if you need me sooner."

Mariah zigzagged though the maze of empty chairs in the clinic waiting room, through the outpatient pharmacy, which was still busy, and turned right to enter the dining hall. "Today's Special" on the chalkboard was meat loaf with mashed potatoes, gravy, and green beans.

Eating at the dining hall aggravated Mariah because she avoided eating meat, and there was never a vegetarian entrée. She ate a vegetarian diet for ethical reasons, lamenting the horrific plight of factory-farmed animals. She loaded her plate with heaping portions of green beans and mashed potatoes—then made up for the lack of a main dish by adding a big piece of gooey, chocolate pudding pie. "All carbs and no protein," she sighed. "I'll be hungry again by ten."

Taking her tray with her to the call room on the fifth floor, Mariah quickly ate her dinner, changed into scrubs, and slipped on her purple plastic clogs. Scrubs were great; they were loose and comfortable like pajamas, and no one could tell if you worked or slept all night.

As Mariah approached the labor and delivery unit, she saw Laura Reynolds standing outside room one. Mariah rushed in to see Penny Reynolds, her private patient from this morning's OB clinic, moving from the ER gurney to the labor bed. She looked childlike in her oversized obstetric hospital gown. Her pregnancy was barely noticeable compared to the big white bandage taped over most of her left thigh. "Hi Penny. I didn't realize *you* were the patient in the ER."

Laura spoke before Penny could answer. "I guess not. We've been in ER all afternoon, and no one from OB has seen her until now."

Sensing the tension, Tracy started taking Penny's vitals. She placed fetal monitors on Penny's pregnant belly. Penny's baby was very premature; Tracy couldn't find the baby's heartbeat. After a moment of searching with the monitor, she looked up at Mariah. Penny and Laura followed Tracy's glance.

"I'll get the ultrasound," Mariah offered and added, "Sometimes it's difficult to find the heartbeat when babies are premature." Turning, Mariah quickly left the room.

Not bothering to hide her frustration, Laura spat, "They didn't have any trouble in the ER."

A moment later, Mariah wheeled the ultrasound machine up to Penny's bedside, plugged it in, and while it was warming up, she squirted gel on Penny's belly.

Mariah tried to take a detailed history without alarming Penny. "Are you having any pain besides your leg? Did you hit your abdomen in the accident? Were you wearing a seatbelt?"

"I was wearing a seatbelt," Penny stammered. "My leg hurts; I don't remember hitting my belly. The baby was active in the emergency room, just not now."

Mariah scanned Penny's baby with the ultrasound, looking for a heartbeat. Penny's belly was small. It should have been easy to see the heart flickering even with the suboptimal "snowy" picture produced by the bedside ultrasound machine. There was no movement. After a very long moment, Mariah focused in on the baby's chest cavity and found the outline of the heart; it was still. The baby had died.

"What's going on?" Penny was getting frightened.

Mariah looked at Penny. "I'm very sorry, but your baby has died."

Laura took over for her sister. "That's impossible. We heard the baby's heartbeat at three o'clock. Do you mean to tell me the baby died while we were waiting for the orthopedics resident to look at Penny's leg?"

The reality of Mariah's words slowly penetrated Penny's brain and then her heart. Her face contorted with grief. She dropped her head into her hands. Her body shuddered as she sobbed without control.

Mariah began to reply to Laura's question when her gaze was drawn to Penny's thigh. Blood was soaking through the bandage.

The bandage had been white and dry fifteen minutes ago when Penny moved off the ER gurney. Now it was soaked with blood and oozing onto the sheets of the labor bed. For a moment Mariah wondered, *Why would Penny's gash start bleeding now?*

Mariah called Tracy over and started pulling the bandage off Penny's leg. The wound wasn't bleeding from a single severed blood vessel. Bright-red blood flowed from every surface of the gash. This was a blood-clotting problem.

Mariah turned to Tracy and began giving orders. "Draw a DIC panel stat and call the blood bank. Find out if she's cross-matched. I'll need four units of blood and cryoprecipitate. Find out how much they have in stock." As Mariah reapplied the bandage to Penny's leg, Penny began to bleed from her IV site.

Laura looked up at Mariah. "What's happening?"

"The baby has died, and Penny is developing disseminated intravascular coagulation—DIC—blood clotting factors are consumed and no longer able to stop bleeding. The accident caused the placenta to pull away from the uterus. This killed the baby; now we might lose Penny. We have to correct the DIC and deliver the baby and placenta from Penny's womb as fast as possible."

Mariah examined Penny's cervix; it was long and closed, meaning a vaginal or "natural" delivery would take hours. Penny didn't have that much time.

Mariah burst into the labor and delivery nurses' station. "Who is the attending doctor on call tonight?"

"Dr. Mettson," Tracy said as she was labeling the tubes of blood and calling the lab to come up to labor and delivery to get her stat blood work. "I paged him."

"I'm calling his house."

Mariah picked up the phone and dialed Dr. David Mettson's home.

"Hello!" David's jovial voice was out of place in the midst of the catastrophe on labor and delivery. Mariah imagined the expression on his face transitioning from "Happy with the wife and kids at dinnertime" to "Oh shit! I'm on my way!"

David called back a few minutes later from his car. He was processing the situation, lining up resources to deal with the inevitable complications, and driving as fast as he dared. "Do you have blood ready? How about fibrinogen? What is her cervical exam? Long and closed? Shit, that means we'll have to do a C-section. Have you called the OR? How about the ICU?"

Multiple transfusions of blood and clotting factors failed to correct Penny's situation. The sudden deceleration force from the car accident had caused a small injury to the placental attachment site along the wall of the uterus. Over the next few hours, the separation grew until the whole placenta detached from the wall of the uterus. This killed Penny's baby and started a deadly chain reaction in her blood. Without clotting factors, Penny's blood flowed freely from any injured blood vessel, and she could bleed to death.

After much debate, the decision was made to

proceed with a C-section. Operating on a patient with no clotting factors is a gamble; the surgery itself can kill the patient. DIC in a pregnant patient presents a difficult dilemma because the lethal consumption of clotting factors can't be corrected until the placenta is removed, and removing the placenta can cause lethal bleeding.

Mariah's heart was pounding in her ears as she held the scalpel above Penny's small but protruding abdomen. The scalpel pulsed between her index finger and thumb as blood rushed through her hands in readiness for the next moment. She quickly scanned the OR; all was ready, blood and clotting factors were infusing. David stood across from her, and her eye caught Laura peering through the observation window. Laura had pulled some strings and obtained permission to watch the surgery through the observation window over the scrub sinks. Slowly, Mariah drew in her breath, cleared her mind of all emotions, and waited for the signal from the anesthesia doctor to begin.

The scalpel flashed under the OR lights, as Mariah began a surgery that might take Penny's life and forever change hers. The situation demanded lightning-fast technique. Mariah incised the skin stretched tightly over the womb; the rest was done bluntly to minimize bleeding. Using only her fingers, she pulled the muscles apart and opened the womb; the baby and placenta were delivered in less than a minute.

Blood poured from the womb, filling the open abdomen and spilling onto the floor. Suction could not keep the surgical field clear of blood. Dr. Gordon pulled the womb up onto the abdomen, above the flow of blood, and swiftly sutured.

"Sew like the wind!" Dr. Haji, her medical school mentor, would say when the bleeding was heavy. Penny was dying. Ten units of blood—more than all the blood in a woman's body—and just as many units of clotting factors were infusing as fast as the IV tubing would allow. Removing the placenta cured the cause of the bleeding, but that did not mean Penny would survive.

Technically, the surgery was uncomplicated, and twenty minutes later Mariah stapled the skin edges closed. The anesthesia doctor was making notes and trying to pump as much fluid and blood components into Penny as he could.

Mariah knew the answer but asked anyway, "How's her BP?"

"It's up to eighty over forty. That's the highest it's been during surgery," the anesthesiologist replied.

Mariah's chest tightened; she knew Penny had lost a lot of blood. Although there was no choice, doing surgery was a hard decision. She wanted to know more. "Any urine output?" This was a measure of how well Penny's body was tolerating the loss of blood. If her kidneys weren't getting blood flow, they wouldn't make urine.

"Nope." His face was grim as he took measures to address Penny's critical hemodynamic status. The C-section was complete. Normally, he would remove the breathing tube, but he was concerned Penny might not be able to breathe on her own yet. "We need to keep her intubated and move her to ICU now."

The OR nurses applied a large pressure bandage to the incision, and Mariah helped move Penny off the OR table to the transport gurney. Penny was small and lightweight. Her small belly still looked pregnant, but the baby and placenta were gone. Mariah checked Penny for bleeding; it had slowed. For an instant, Mariah felt some relief.

Once in the ICU, Penny's care was transferred to the ICU specialist. He worked with the anesthesia doctor to confirm Penny's ventilator settings and IV medications. It would take at least an hour to get Penny settled before attempting any further action, like extubation.

Mariah went back to labor and delivery; it was quiet. One patient with preterm contractions was being evaluated by Dr. Todd Woods, the second-year OB resident on call with Mariah. He was busy writing up her admission paperwork when Mariah walked into the labor and delivery nurses' station.

"Hi, Mariah! I don't think this patient is in preterm labor, but I'm going to observe her for a few hours just to make sure." He was a good resident; Mariah was glad he was on call with her tonight.

Dr. David Mettson walked into labor and delivery just as Mariah sat down. This was David's first opportunity to discuss the circumstances surrounding Penny's care since the surgery. She knew he'd have some questions.

"Mariah, when did Penny show up in the ER?" David sat down next to her at the nurses' station.

"I was paged around 2:30 p.m.," Mariah replied.

David nodded. "The ER director told me she arrived by ambulance at 12:30 p.m. When did you evaluate her in the ER?"

Mariah leaned back in her chair, crossed her arms defensively, and began to recount the events. "Dr. Anthony reported her condition was stable, the fetal heart tones were normal, and that Dr. Taylor, the orthopedics resident, was going to take her to the OR to treat a gash in her thigh. I chose to wait and see the patient after her leg wound was treated in the OR." She took a moment to explain her actions. "She was very preterm, and her only problem seemed to be the gash on her leg."

Mariah continued, "Unfortunately, they did *not* check the baby's heartbeat again after 3:00 p.m., and I was *not* notified when Dr. Taylor changed his mind and treated her wound in the ER. She arrived on labor and delivery at about 5:30 p.m., which is when I saw her. Penny looked fine, initially. The bandage on her leg was clean and dry when we started her evaluation. Then we couldn't find the fetal heartbeat. Bedside ultrasound diagnosed fetal demise, and then I noticed her leg wound was bleeding and soaking through the bandage. I removed the bandage to check her wound, and she started bleeding from everywhere. That's when I ordered the DIC panel and called you. It happened that fast."

David was visibly shaken by this case. "I never would have gone home tonight if I knew about this patient." Although his specialty was gynecologic oncology, as an attending in BAMC's OB-GYN resident training program, he managed obstetric cases when on call. "What are her recent vital signs? Has she had any urine output yet?"

"The ICU hasn't called me," Mariah answered. "Let's go back down to the ICU and see how she's doing."

David nodded. They walked down the hallway together in silence. Not all attending doctors worked this collegially with their chief residents. David was still relatively young, energetic, and idealistic. He remembered what it was like to be a resident.

Entering the ICU, it was obvious something was not right. The ICU specialist saw them enter and hurried around the busy nurses' station toward them, yelling, "Here they are, don't bother paging them!" His stethoscope fell off his neck as he approached. Although his specialty was critical care, managing Penny's complicated case was making him nervous. His bald spot was shining with sweat.

"Your patient is having trouble maintaining her blood pressure. I think her abdomen is filling with blood," he said and quickly replaced his stethoscope.

"I placed two suction drains in her abdomen. Are the drains putting out any blood?" Mariah asked.

The ICU specialist spread his feet, standing with his hands on his hips. "No, but her blood pressure is dropping, and her urine output is next to nothing. I think you have to take her back to the OR right away, or we'll lose her."

David said softly, "We might still lose her if we go back to the OR,"

Mariah scanned Penny's ICU room for Laura. She was pressed against the back wall as a nurse drew blood, and an X-ray technician took a chest X-ray. Their eyes met, and Laura came to life. She grabbed her purse and made her way out through the tangle of machines and tubing, into the hallway to speak with Mariah.

"How is she?" Laura's eyes searched Mariah for unspoken clues.

Mariah was direct. "Not good. We think she's still bleeding. We have to take her back to the OR."

Laura's face fell. This was not supposed to be happening. Penny was young, healthy, and talking about baby names in the ER a few hours ago. How could she be this sick so fast?

"OK, when will you do that? In the morning?" It was getting late, and Penny had already been through so much.

Mariah shook her head. "Immediately. Penny's life depends on it. We must act fast. I want you to know that Penny's situation is not good. Her chances are only fifty-fifty. We're working as hard as we can." Mariah reached out to touch Laura's arm in support.

Laura pulled her arm back. "Now you're sorry! Where were you when she was waiting in the ER all afternoon?" Laura's eyes narrowed with hatred, as if somehow this whole catastrophe was deliberately orchestrated against her. "Maybe if you had seen her sooner this all could have been prevented."

Her words echoed thoughts in Mariah's head. But Mariah knew that nothing could have prevented this catastrophe, which was now a real-life nightmare.

"I'm sorry," was all Mariah could say as she turned to go to the OR.

Back in the OR, the lights were bright and the monitors were beeping. Penny was still unconscious and intubated from her first surgery. Her belly was scrubbed again and draped with blue sheets. The bruised and stapled abdomen was painted again with Betadine, and Mariah noticed it was swollen larger than before the C-section.

She and David scrubbed, gowned, and began undoing their work. The staple remover extracted the staples from Penny's skin in the same manner one would remove staples from sheets of paper. Next, the white sutures holding the abdominal tissues together were snipped. A horrifying gush of blood burst from the wound. The bleeding quickly overwhelmed the suction device, obscuring their view of the surgical field. Blood flowed over the drapes onto the operating room floor, soaking Mariah's and David's booties for the second time that night.

Mariah felt a sensation of panic. It began at the back of her head, squeezed her neck, and made her hands start to cramp. She wasn't sure what to do next.

The release of blood caused Penny's blood pressure to initially improve. For an instant, Mariah fantasized that Penny would survive, get better, and go back to work. But that brief, bright moment faded as anesthesia called for the code cart. Penny's blood pressure became undetectable, and although a heart rhythm appeared on the monitors, she had no pulse. Electromechanical dissociation was tricking the monitors into "beeping" a heart rhythm while Penny was silently slipping away.

Chest compressions, medications, fluids, blood products—nothing could reverse the bleeding and revive this young woman who, a few hours ago, was overjoyed to hear her unborn baby's heartbeat.

Chapter Three

The experience of losing an obstetric patient is surreal. Like the patient's soul, the doctor feels transported above the patient's body and looks down upon the commotion below as if in a dream. The doctor and patient each pray, "This can't be happening to me." For an instant, the dying patient realizes how much the doctor cared for her. And as the soul of the dying patient departs, it takes a little piece of the doctor's soul with it.

It was midnight when Mariah finished dictating the operative reports for Penny's two surgeries. The hallways were dark, and a cold silence filled the void as she waited for the elevator. Mariah felt drained, without a tear to cry or a voice to shout.

She realized that she hadn't spoken to Emery since breakfast. She thought about calling him now, but knew it would be unreasonable to wake him at this hour and hope to have a meaningful conversation.

Instead, she decided to check in with the nurses on labor and delivery before lying down in the call room. Mariah looked around hopefully for companionship as she entered labor and delivery's nurses' station. "Hello!" she called softly.

Mona and Denise appeared saying, "Hello" in unison. Mariah liked working with them. They were BAMC's most experienced night-shift nurses.

Denise bustled up to Mariah and gave her a big

hug. "Honey, are you all right?"

Mariah nodded but her face looked dejected.

Denise continued, "Everything here is under control. Our preterm labor patient stopped contracting; we sent her home. Dr. Woods is admitting a twenty-year-old patient in early labor with her first baby. She's only two centimeters dilated and insists she's in too much pain with her contractions to walk around any more." Denise winked. "Her baby looked great on the monitor, and her vital signs were stable. Dr. Woods is going to manage her pain with morphine until active labor begins."

Mona looked at Mariah. "You look down. I hope you don't beat yourself up over that case. The way I heard it, there was nothing you could've done to save that girl. Her time was up the moment her car hit the guardrail."

Mariah poured a cup of coffee. "That may be true, but I doubt Dr. Halligan will agree when I present this case at Morning Report. Someone will have to take the blame for Penny's death. It's going to be me."

Mona shook her head. "That's ridiculous! The orthopedics resident never even called you; I heard that from the ER nurse. She told me Dr. Taylor was going to take the patient to the OR and then he got too busy, so he changed his mind and bandaged her leg in the ER. Very uncomfortable for the patient too; it made the ER nurses mad."

Mariah cringed knowing that Penny's final hours were made worse by cleaning her leg wound without anesthesia. "Wish it were that simple. I doubt if anyone is going to see it that way."

Mona smiled. "Don't worry. Dr. Mettson was there. He'll back you up."

It was after 2:00 a.m. "I'm going to lie down. Call me if you need me." Mariah walked down the hall toward the call room.

It felt great to lie down on the call room bed after such an awful day. Her body was exhausted, but her mind would not turn off. Over and over, she replayed the events in her head and asked the same questions: What could she have done differently? If she went to the ER earlier, would Penny still be alive? The abruption of the placenta was due to the car accident. Once the abruption occurred, DIC depleted Penny's clotting factors, putting her life in jeopardy.

Penny's baby was too premature to survive outside the womb and would not be delivered except to save Penny's life. If Penny's baby had been monitored continuously while she was in the ER, they would have known when the abruption occurred. And though nothing could be done to save the baby, Mariah believed it was better to know the baby's status. Penny still could have developed DIC and died.

Continuous fetal monitoring in the ER was the only omission Mariah could find in Penny's medical management prior to the C-section. She made a mental note to discuss requiring fetal monitoring for all pregnant trauma patients while they wait in the ER. Having solved the dilemma, Mariah finally fell asleep.

Her beeper went off a few minutes later. She rubbed her eyes, got out of bed to reach the phone, and punched the number for labor and delivery. "This is Dr. Gordon."

Dr. Todd Woods had managed labor and delivery without help while Mariah and Dr. Mettson operated and reoperated on Penny. Mariah knew he wouldn't call her unless he had no choice. "Hi, Mariah. This is Todd. I'm calling from labor and delivery. You know that patient I admitted in labor? Well, she's four centimeters dilated now, and I'm pretty sure her baby is breech."

Mariah couldn't believe her bad luck. "I'll be right there." She was so tired that her body ached, and all she wanted to do was go back to sleep. A breech baby at four centimeters was not an emergency; Mariah knew she could rest another minute or two, but she was afraid she might fall back asleep.

As an intern, she once answered a page and then fell asleep again without ever really waking up. Hours later, when she passed the nurses' station to get coffee, they asked her what took her so long to get there. Mariah was shocked to learn she had answered the phone and given orders without being completely awake. Since then, whenever Mariah was paged from a sound sleep, she got out of bed and put both feet on the floor before making any medical decisions.

She sat on the side of her bed and shivered with cold. *It must be around 4:00 a.m.*, she thought. *I always get cold at this hour of the morning.*

Reaching into her locker, she pulled out her favorite sweater—a soft, bright-pink cardigan purchased from a flea market downtown. It made her feel better just wearing it underneath her white lab coat. The army required all sweaters to be black, but Mariah liked the pink. She only wore it on labor and delivery in the middle of the night, when she could go from patient to patient wrapped in her warm, fuzzy sweater. Most of her patients smiled when they saw it, although the hard-core, active duty patients never liked it much.

Mariah pulled the sweater tightly around her shoulders, slipped her feet into her purple clogs, and walked out of the call room before she could think twice about lying down again.

Labor and delivery was busy. Two new patients had arrived in addition to the patient with the breech baby. One patient was sick with the flu and needed IV hydration. The other patient had a fight with her husband, and when he stomped out the door, she developed pains in her belly. The key to treating her successfully was to determine if she was having pain from a physical problem or from an emotional one.

The laboring patient's baby was indeed breech. A C-section delivery was risky for the mother, but vaginal breech deliveries were associated with increased risk for both the mother and baby. C-section was the safest plan for this patient.

Mariah called the OR, anesthesia, and then David to let him know she was operating again that night. David had stayed at the hospital and was sleeping in a call room.

She told him, "You don't need to come to the OR. I just wanted to make you aware that a C-section was taking place."

The C-section was uncomplicated, and the baby was born healthy—a welcome contrast to earlier events. Morning Report loomed ahead.

Checking in with both the nurses and her team of residents confirmed the patients on the OB floor were all doing well. Armed with a coffee and a breakfast taco from the truck outside the ER, Mariah felt as prepared as possible.

Unfortunately, buying the taco and coffee made her a minute late for Morning Report. Mariah quietly entered the back of the Morning Report conference room and stood with the interns while Dr. Nelson, chief of the OB-GYN department, called the group to order. Dr. Nelson was a quiet, genteel, old-school doctor who rarely spoke, but when he did, everyone listened. Seeing Mariah, he motioned for her to come to the front.

Mariah cleared her throat. "Last night we had two C-sections. One was for a breech presentation. The patient was twenty years old, pregnant with her first child, and just three days shy of her due date. The patient was initially admitted in early labor, and once her cervix dilated to four centimeters, she was noted to be breech and taken to the OR for a C-section. The baby had a normal fetal heart rate tracing, weighed seven pounds, six ounces, the Apgars were eight and nine, and there were no complications." Mariah took a sip of coffee.

"The second case was a twenty-one-year-old active duty specialist at twenty-four weeks gestation. She was seen in the clinic yesterday morning for a routine OB visit and, sometime around 12:30 p.m., was involved in a high-speed motor vehicle accident. She was going about fifty miles per hour on Highway 10 when a car sideswiped her. She was brought to our ER and on admission had stable vitals, normal fetal heart tones, and a pretty big gash in her upper left thigh. I was paged around 2:00 p.m. and told that orthopedics was going to treat the gash in the OR. Since her vitals were stable and the baby's heartbeat was normal, I elected to evaluate her after the orthopedic doctors treated her leg wound. At 5:30 p.m. she arrived on labor and delivery—she had not gone to the OR; her thigh wound was cleaned and bandaged in the ER.

"Upon arrival to labor and delivery, the patient was comfortable and the bandage on her left thigh was clean and dry. She seemed fine and moved herself from the ER gurney to the labor bed. Her vitals were stable, but we could not find the fetal heartbeat. Bedside ultrasound confirmed fetal death, and placental abruption was suspected. Within minutes, the patient began to bleed from her leg wound, soaking her bandage. Close inspection of the wound showed bleeding from all surfaces. When her IV site also began to bleed, DIC was suspected, and blood work confirmed the diagnosis. A decision was made to perform a stat C-section under general anesthesia."

Dr. Halligan interrupted. "Did you correct her

bleeding problem before you started the surgery?"

Mariah replied, "We tried, but transfusing several units of blood and clotting factors failed to correct her DIC. We decided that the only way to fix the problem was to evacuate the uterus." She looked from Dr. Halligan to Dr. Mettson.

Dr. Halligan shot back, "Well, I never heard of anything more ridiculous in my whole life. No wonder she died; you took her to the OR with DIC!"

Mariah, wondering when David was going to speak up and support her, continued, "Her blood coagulation lab tests were normal, but her fibrinogen-split products were off the charts, indicating her situation was worsening. We felt our best chance was to get in and out of the OR as fast as possible."

Dr. Halligan looked around the room. "Who is 'we'?" Attending doctors and residents glanced nervously at each other.

Dr. David Mettson finally spoke up. "I was notified about this case as the patient was going into the OR."

Oh great, Mariah thought, *now David's going to throw me under the bus and make the whole thing look like it was my idea.*

David continued, "But I do agree with Mariah. The only chance for survival was to do a C-section and remove the baby and placenta from her uterus."

Crossing his arms, Dr. Halligan asked, "So, how did it go?" Then he sat back with a smug smile on his face;

he already knew the answer to his question.

"Well, the C-section was uneventful…" Mariah began.

"Uneventful!" Dr. Halligan stood up.

Dr. Nelson held his hand up for seated silence.

Mariah was getting shaken. "I meant it was not complicated by any injuries to nearby organs. The bleeding was extremely heavy. We placed drains, closed her, and moved her to the ICU. An hour later, her vitals became unstable, and her clotting factors remained abnormal, indicating she was still bleeding internally, likely from her uterus. We took the patient back to the OR to try to stop her bleeding. We knew she was at high risk for mortality but felt we had no choice."

The residents in the room were silent, internalizing the scenario and hoping something similar would never happen to them.

Mariah continued, "Back in the OR, the patient's blood pressure rebounded briefly and then dropped. She coded as soon as we opened her up, and we couldn't bring her back."

Dr. Nelson broke the silence. "Well, you can say what you want about this patient's management, but in my opinion, the moment she developed DIC, she was in trouble. Why didn't we see her sooner?"

Mariah took a deep breath and again tried to justify why she decided to wait until the leg wound was treated before seeing the patient in the ER.

"Guess you won't make that mistake again." Dr.

Nelson's comment concluded the discussion.

The words stung, and Mariah felt she was unfairly judged, but instead of arguing, she just nodded and moved back to her place at the back of the room among the interns. All plans for recommending fetal monitoring in the ER for any future OB patients disappeared.

Mariah just wanted to be alone somewhere quiet. Caring for patients all day in OB clinic seemed like an insurmountable task. She tried to think about something good—Emery was home and waiting for her to return! She planned to call him the minute they were dismissed from Morning Report.

Chapter Four

Mariah rode the elevator down to the OB clinic but instead of seeing her clinic patients, she closed the door to her office and dialed her home phone number. Emery visited for long weekends as often as he could. Mariah usually had to work one night during his visit; her difficult schedule was an obstacle they hoped would disappear after residency. After five rings, Mariah began to wonder what Emery was doing while she struggled to recover from one of the worst nights of her life. After eight rings, she hung up, sad and annoyed that he was not there to answer the phone.

Emery was shopping for a surprise dinner when Mariah called. He bought her favorite dish—macaroni and cheese, a bottle of wine, and a fruit tart for dessert. Unlike Mariah, he was not a vegetarian and selected steak and a few potatoes for his dinner. While standing in the checkout line, he picked up the current edition of *Aviation Week*.

In college, Emery wanted to join the Air Force and be a pilot, but his eyesight eliminated him from flight school. Undaunted, he pursued a career in law and indulged his interest in aviation with flight lessons. Emery enjoyed ground school and was collecting flying time for his first solo flight.

He was obsessed with anything that could fly, read several aviation magazines, and flew model airplanes. San

Antonio was an idyllic city to visit because it was home to Lackland, Randolph, Kelly, and Brooks Air Force bases. Fighter planes and cargo jet contrails crisscrossed the sky, and every local store had some sort of aviation mementos for sale. Bookstores were full of interesting flight books, and even the food stores had a complete inventory of aviation magazines.

The cover article was on the FAA's success at decreasing plane crashes by using a team-oriented approach called crew resource management (CRM). CRM grew out of an analysis of the United Airlines Flight 173 crash in 1978, where the plane ran out of fuel while the flight crew was troubleshooting a landing-gear problem. CRM was a set of training procedures that focused on interpersonal communication, leadership, and decision-making in the cockpit. The article noted that CRM was improving safety in the airline industry and was required training for both civilian and Department of Defense aviators. Emery was fascinated by any organizational approach that could bring about a safer flying experience; he put the magazine in the cart to peruse later while he waited for Mariah to come home.

Mariah was exhausted and no matter how hard she tried to concentrate, her mind just wanted to sleep. The minutes dragged, and each patient was complicated; nothing was fast or easy. She drifted off during a patient's appointment. The patient was describing her latest in a long line of social problems, including her boyfriend's unemployment and infidelity, when Mariah fell asleep. She awoke instantly when her head bobbed, and noticed her pen had traced a crooked line down the page as her arm slid off the desk.

"I'm so sorry," Mariah tried to explain. "I really am interested in what you're saying, it's just that I was on call last night and hardly slept. Why don't we get a social work consult to see if that will help you with some of your personal relationship issues."

At lunch, Mariah was starving. She craved macaroni and cheese, but the dining hall was serving roast turkey with stuffing, mashed potatoes, gravy, and green beans. She ate two large helpings of potatoes and green beans, knowing she would regret it; a full stomach always made her sleepy.

Strong, black coffee usually helped, but today nothing short of chocolate could keep her awake. *No wonder we gain weight in residency*, she thought and made a mental note to go for a run tomorrow. Someone on labor and delivery always had a stash of emergency chocolate, and Mariah went straight to the elevator and pushed five.

"Hey, Mariah!" Bernice called across the labor and delivery nursing station.

Bernice Martinez had a friendly, energetic character. As a civilian employee, she was allowed to wear scrubs made of pretty, printed fabric, and she often put bright clips or barrettes in her bleached-blond hair. The effect was warm and friendly, and she always had a big smile for her patients.

She gave Mariah a hug. "Honey, are you OK? I heard you had a bad night, but I want you to know that you're still number one in my book."

Without the constraints of army rank and hierarchy, she felt at ease calling everyone by either their given names, or any other term of endearment she felt applied. One afternoon, Dr. Nelson happened to be walking past labor and delivery when Bernice called out, "Dr. Nelson! Honey, can you please help me get this labor bed unlocked so I can wheel this patient down the hall, or we will have ourselves a baby right here in the hallway." Even Dr. Nelson could not resist the command-like quality of her Louisiana southern drawl; without a word of protest, he kicked the pedal to unlock the bed and helped wheel the patient down to the delivery room.

Bernice's husband, Manuel, was a major in the US Army Medical Service Corps. He ran the troop clinic for the training division that was attached to BAMC. They had two middle school–aged children and were a typical army family, moving every two years when Major Martinez's assignment changed. Bernice was accustomed to making new friends and getting a new job every time they moved. She always kept a stash of chocolate to help with tough times. She took one look at Mariah's face, reached into the file cabinet drawer where she stored her purse, and produced a handful of fun-sized chocolate bars and a supersized Snickers bar.

"What can I offer to help you feel better, darlin'?" Bernice placed the candy on the nursing station countertop, and Mariah's eyes scanned the chocolate bars.

"Do you mind if I take the big Snickers?" She reached for it like a kid at Halloween.

"Go on, and another one for later this afternoon. Now shouldn't you be down in clinic?" Bernice ushered Mariah out of labor and delivery toward the elevator.

The chocolate bars worked their magic, and before Mariah knew it, all her clinic patients were seen. It was Friday afternoon and, with the exception of seeing her OB ward patients on Saturday and Sunday morning, she was off all weekend. Mariah tried calling Emery one more time from the call room as she gathered her things. By now she was tired and cranky.

The phone rang several times before Emery answered. "Hello!" He sounded happy.

Mariah wished she could feel that way, too. "Hi, it's me. I'm leaving now. Sorry I didn't call last night, but I did try earlier today. Where were you?"

"That must have been while I was out shopping." Emery almost dropped the phone, and Mariah could tell he was picking up the apartment as he spoke. "I got us great food for dinner. How was your night? You sound beat."

Mariah almost cried just thinking about it. "I'm exhausted. It was one of the worst nights of my life. I'll tell you about it when I get home." Last night's events still seemed unimaginable.

"OK. I'll see you soon. Take your time and be careful driving home. Love you."

Mariah swallowed her tears. "I love you too."

Driving home after a long night on call was dangerous. Mariah's commute was thirty minutes, assuming Irving didn't stall along the way. It was boring and monotonous, a perfect setup for a tired driver to fall asleep while at the wheel. The usual tricks, chewing gum and loud music, didn't work tonight. She tried to keep herself interested in the surroundings by reading every billboard, then counting the exits, but she could tell she was drifting off, forgetting which exit she had just passed. She tried making herself relive every moment of the prior night, but her thoughts were like clouds drifting around the difficult parts. She opened the windows, but the wind blew her hair in her face, making her squint, and tempting her to close her eyes. Instead, she closed the windows and turned the A/C on high.

How long have I been driving? It feels like I should be there already. She looked at the next exit and realized she was only halfway home. She stared hard ahead at the road and tried to keep the car in the middle of her lane.

BUMP, BUMP! Irving lurched to the left as Mariah opened her eyes. Her car was running along the left edge of the lane where the highway's reflectors protruded along the white line, bumping her tires and jostling her brain back to consciousness. For a split second, Mariah had fallen asleep while driving 65 mph. She was dangerously close to the cement barricade in the center of the highway. Mariah panicked and swerved back onto the highway—without those reflectors, she would have hit the barricade and rolled over into the oncoming traffic. Adrenaline surged through her body, making her skin tingle and her heart pound.

Exiting the highway, Mariah rolled down her window and leaned her head out, letting the wind wash over her face. She wished the wind could wash away the images from last night too, but nothing could do that— except maybe a shot of scotch.

She parked Irving outside her apartment building and looked up at the yellow light coming from her kitchen window on the second floor. The glow was warm and inviting as she climbed the cement staircase. Once she was inside, Emery gave her a big hug, kissed her lightly, and took her bag and briefcase. She thanked him and fell into her old leather recliner.

"You look beat." Emery smiled as he handed her a glass of scotch with a few ice cubes. Emery sat on the couch and waited for her to speak.

The silence was more than Mariah could bear, so she began her story. "Last night I lost a patient. Not just one patient, but her baby, too. And she wasn't just any patient; she was Laura Reynolds's sister. Penny was in a car accident. Her baby died while she waited in the ER to be seen by orthopedics. By the time she got to labor and delivery, she was in DIC and started to bleed from everywhere. We took her to the OR and tried to save her, but she died."

Mariah continued, "But the worst part was when Laura blamed me. Her accusations about Penny's care were scathing." Mariah started to sob. "And I'm not sure I disagree with her."

Emery sprang up and put his arms around her, folding her into his chest.

All the emotion and self-doubt Mariah had suppressed all day came rushing out. "I feel like a failure. I tried to do everything right, and it all went wrong. I just want to be a good doctor."

"You're a great doctor." Emery smoothed Mariah's hair off her wet face and handed her the napkin from his drink.

"You're the only person who believes that today." She blew her nose loudly. "How could you go out with Laura in high school?" Mariah needed to digress from her story. "My medical assistant calls her 'evil.' I know she's beautiful, but her personality is venomous; it's hard to believe anyone could be attracted to her."

Emery attempted to defend himself. "It was high school, Mariah; personality didn't matter." He smiled sheepishly. "Forget about Laura Reynolds. She never let a comment or conflict end without the last word. She used her good looks to attract any boy that someone else liked, including me."

Mariah stared at Emery. "Really?"

"She used me to get even with my old girlfriend. They hated each other. One day, at a football game, Laura approached me and told me my girlfriend was cheating on me. Before I knew it, *we* were kissing, and my girlfriend caught us. A few weeks later, Laura broke it off."

Emery continued, "I think Laura had a rough childhood. Her mother was a real piece of work, emotionally unstable and an alcoholic. Maybe Laura made up for a lack of love by punishing her enemies and collecting trophies like me!" He smiled and tried to coax Mariah out of her sadness.

"I find that hard to believe." Anxious to change the subject, she added, "What have you been up to today?"

Emery replied, "Working. I wrote a brief after going shopping for dinner. And, while standing in line at the grocery store, I found an article in an aviation magazine that might interest you." He placed the *Aviation Week* magazine in Mariah's lap.

"Aircraft safety is a big problem for the aviation industry, and root cause analysis determined that most mistakes were caused by errors in communication. They used a team-based approach to decrease communication mistakes, and the rate of aircraft crashes and near misses declined dramatically. Maybe a similar approach would work in health care."

Mariah picked up the magazine and tried to sound interested. "Really?" She didn't want to talk about health care anymore that night. "I'm looking forward to going to David's party on Sunday. Aren't you?"

Emery lost all his enthusiasm. "Oh yeah. A room full of docs, their spouses, and kids is my favorite kind of party. And not just any doctors...ob-gyns! The conversation will go from delivering babies to hysterectomies and vaginal procedures. No one will know or care what I do for a living. The conversation is always all about them. No offense, but as a group, doctors are very self-centered."

Mariah laughed. "Really? I'm sorry, what did you say again? I was too busy focusing on myself to hear what you said." She had to admit Emery had a point, and it felt good to laugh a little. "What's for dinner? I'm starved."

Chapter Five

Saturday morning was clear and sunny. Mariah awoke peacefully, cuddled next to Emery, and fantasized about spending the whole day together in bed. Ten minutes later, the alarm clock, beeping like a car alarm, extinguished her fantasy, reminding her that she wanted to go for a run before making rounds at the hospital.

In medical school, Mariah ran every day to relieve stress, but residency changed all that. Long hours at the hospital wore her out, and now running felt more like a chore. Memories of endless, effortless miles quickly gave way to the reality of a slower, plodding pace infused with pain and fatigue. Mariah desperately wanted to maintain her fitness, but the demands of her profession made that practically impossible. She did what she could, running when time and strength allowed.

Medicine is like a jealous lover, demanding every waking moment of your life. Mariah sacrificed much during her residency training; she worked nights, weekends, and holidays, and she gave up her athletic lifestyle to allow time for study and work. Occasionally putting her vegetarian beliefs aside, opting to eat meat at the hospital dining hall in lieu of going without a balanced meal on call, she wondered how much of the "old Mariah" would remain after residency training. Now that the final month of her residency approached, she felt relief and a sense of pride. She made it! Even her relationship with

Emery was still strong.

When she returned, Emery poured her a mug full of steamy, black coffee. "How was your run?"

Still panting and sweating, Mariah tried to slow her breathing. "Hard. Glad I did it." She sank to the floor with her coffee and stretched her hamstrings.

Smiling hopefully, like a child asking for a cookie, Emery asked, "There's an air show at Randolph Air Force Base this afternoon. Want to go?"

Mariah sipped her coffee while twisting to stretch her back. "I thought we were going tubing on the river up in Gruene this afternoon?"

Seeing the look on his face, she added, "But OK! That would be fun." She knew how much Emery loved airplanes and anything related to aviation, and couldn't begrudge him the chance to see an air show, especially after he waited for her all day yesterday.

Then she added quickly, "Do you want to come with me to the hospital this morning while I make rounds? That way we can eat lunch downtown on the river walk and then go to the air show together."

"Sure. I have some briefs I can work on while you see your patients. Is there a desk I can use?"

"You can use my desk in the residents' office." Mariah got up, refilled her coffee, and walked toward the shower.

Emery called after her, "I hear the Thunderbirds may do a flyby at the air show! They're temporarily stationed here in San Antonio at Lackland Air Force

Base."

Mariah looked back over her shoulder and smiled a little too enthusiastically. "Really? I can't wait." Then she closed the bathroom door.

Emery, not sure if she was serious or not, decided to follow her into the bathroom and join her for a shower.

Emery hoped to marry Mariah and build a happy life together. He grew up on the Main Line in Pennsylvania, and home life for him was always happy. Mariah had not experienced an idyllic childhood, and felt it was essential to be successful in her career before she could commit to anyone. She needed to be self-sufficient. They talked of marriage, but Mariah always brought up one more challenge that needed to be completed: first medical school, then residency.

Now that her residency was almost complete, they agreed to move to a mutually acceptable location: Fort Benning, Georgia. Fort Benning's hospital, Mitchell Army Community Hospital (MACH), needed an ob-gyn, and Emery planned to transfer to a law firm in Atlanta recommended by one of the partners at his law office.

At the hospital, Mariah was all business. She showed Emery where the residents' office was located and then went to see her patients on the OB ward. Emery quickly installed himself at Mariah's desk and was busy reading a deposition when he heard someone enter.

"Emery Davison! Is that you?" Laura crossed the office casually, acting as though she often visited the OB-

GYN residents' office.

"Hello, Laura." He stood up and stiffly offered a handshake.

Laura turned his gesture into an affectionate hug. Emery felt embarrassed and off-balance embracing across Mariah's desk.

Laura pulled up a chair and sat down next to Mariah's desk. "How have you been?"

Laura's attractive and commanding appearance caught Emery by surprise. He felt awkward and lost his composure. Memories of their high school romance flooded his brain.

"Great! How about you?" The inappropriateness of his remark was intensified by the fact that Laura's sister had just died.

"I've been better. My sister's death has me thinking about life and how precious it is. I remember the good times we had together. Do you ever think about those days? Skipping class in high school together..."

"No. I mean, occasionally. But, almost never." Emery needed to regain his composure.

He cleared his mind and his throat and tried again. "That was a long time ago, Laura." Emery faked a chuckle. "Were we ever really that young and naïve?"

"I remember everything." Laura smiled. "Even the secrets we shared about your ex-girlfriend."

Feeling cornered and threatened, Emery decided he should leave. Rising from his chair, "I have to go. It's been nice catching up with you, Laura."

"Don't go! We should get reacquainted, don't you think?" Laura leaned close and touched Emery's hand.

Emery looked down at her hand. He pulled his hand back and jammed it into his pocket.

"I don't know what you're talking about. We were kids back then. I'm with Mariah now." Softer, almost pleading, Emery added, "I'm sorry for the loss of your sister. Mariah feels just awful about the whole thing. Why don't you go easy on her, OK? For me and whatever relationship you remember that we had." Emery tried to smile.

Laura's eyes narrowed. "You're asking *me*, the victim, to give the doctor responsible for Penny's death a break? How can you even be involved with her?" Laura slammed her hand on Mariah's desk.

Stunned by Laura's outburst, Emery regained his composure. "I love Mariah."

Laura smiled and her pale-blue eyes flashed as she too regained her composure. "Of course you do. And I'm sure Mariah loves you too." She leaned over and kissed him on the cheek, like an old friend. "Good-bye, Emery." She walked out of the office. A faint fragrance from high school lingered in the deserted office.

Emery slowly sat back down. The phone on the desk rang, and he answered, "Residents' office, Dr. Gordon's desk."

"I'm almost done! Want to meet me in the parking lot in ten minutes?" Mariah sounded happy, and Emery didn't want to spoil the mood.

"All right! I'll meet you at Irving in ten." He hung up the phone and sat for a moment, rubbing the lipstick off his cheek. Laura's formidable presence still filled his mind, mingling with vivid memories of their teenage romance.

The air show was crowded, and the parking lot for Randolph Air Force Base was full. Mariah and Emery had to park several blocks away, along a side street in a nearby housing development. Heat waves swirled up from the pavement as they walked back toward the main entrance.

The sergeant in the guardhouse waved them through as Mariah flashed her US Army ID card. Admission was three dollars, and sodas and water bottles were for sale in large tubs filled with ice next to the ticket counters. All the seats were taken, so they found a patch of grass beside the tarmac and sat down, legs outstretched, leaning back on their arms to view the sky. A loudspeaker crackled to life, and after a brief welcome, a woman began to sing "The Star-Spangled Banner." Everyone who was able rose to stand at attention or salute the American flag flying from the air traffic control tower. The Thunderbirds roared overhead, leaving a red-white-and-blue smoke trail across the sky. The patriotism was palpable throughout the crowd as everyone cheered and took their seats.

Emery was enthralled as the planes demonstrated the latest in aviation capabilities. Mariah was more impressed with how rapidly the temperature climbed to one hundred and went in search of something to drink. She returned to the ticket booth area, but the water bottles were gone, and the tubs held only a few sodas floating in dirty ice water. Wiping off two cans of Coke, she turned and almost collided with Bernice walking hand in hand with her two children.

Mariah was happy to see a familiar face. "Hi, Bernice! Are these your kids?"

Bernice was flushed from the heat. "Hey, Mariah! This is Antonio and Tanja."

"Hi, guys. This is a great air show, isn't it?" Mariah smiled at Antonio.

"Yeah, it's cool," he replied.

"The Thunderbirds were very cool!" Tanja added.

Bernice injected her own opinion. "We've been here for hours and the heat is getting to me." The kids waved as they walked past the deserted ticket booth in search of their car.

Mariah walked back to join Emery, who was completely engrossed. F-16 fighters streaked down from the sky, touched the runway briefly, and then pulled straight up into the sky. The engine blast was deafening and blew dusty wind everywhere. She handed him a Coke.

"Thanks, hon." Emery liked to call Mariah "hon," and she didn't mind it too much. Using terms of endearment in a relationship was new for Mariah.

Mariah settled back on the grass, pretending to watch the rest of the air show, lost in her own thoughts. Tomorrow's party at David's house would be an interesting event. Jared, his three-month-old son, was being christened, and David had invited the whole OB-GYN department to celebrate.

Mariah admired David. He seemed to have everything she wanted: family, career, and happiness. His wife, Joanna, had a son from a previous marriage, and together they had a daughter and now a new baby boy. This party was a perfect chance for Mariah to see David at home and observe his family interactions.

Mariah had grown up in a family fractured by divorce and conflict. She wanted a better life for herself and future family. As a child, Mariah had dreamed of being a surgeon. Her self-esteem and personal identity were tied to her vision of a confident, successful doctor in a long white lab coat.

But Mariah wanted more than just a career; she wanted a happy family life. Her mother was a smart businesswoman but failed miserably when it came to personal relationships. After divorcing Mariah's father, she had worked hard to provide a financially stable home. After a long workday, there was no time or energy left for affection. Mariah had filled the void by overachieving academically. She hoped that observing David's family would provide clues about how to achieve a successful personal life away from the everyday stress of medicine.

The air show ended with an explosion of fireworks, and Mariah couldn't wait to get back to the quiet of the apartment. Chinese food, a few beers, and lying in each other's arms watching a movie was all she remembered before she fell asleep.

On Sunday morning, Jenna pulled up to Mariah's apartment at 8:00 a.m. They occasionally carpooled to work, and this morning Mariah and Jenna both planned to make rounds early before going to David's party. Mariah, wearing a navy skirt and pink blouse, climbed into Jenna's pickup truck. Uniforms weren't mandatory on weekends, and it was always fun to wear "real" clothes and see what everyone else wore off duty.

"Good morning!" Mariah looked at Jenna's jeans and T-shirt, with *Love an Artist* written across it, and asked, "Aren't you going to David's party?" Jenna's husband, Floyd, was an artist who made intricate prints on a large printing press in their garage.

"Of course, I wouldn't miss it. But first Floyd and I have to hang one of his new prints in a gallery downtown. We might be a little late."

"Emery is picking me up at eleven thirty. I hope I can finish seeing all my patients by then." Mariah checked her watch and pulled her stethoscope out of her purse, hanging it around her neck.

Once at the hospital, she went straight to work seeing postpartum patients, discharging new mothers, and ensuring the high-risk pregnant patients were stable. The morning flew by, and Mariah tried hard to stay on time.

At 11:30 a.m., Emery drove up to the hospital entrance and coaxed Irving's obstinate gearshift into park. He knew Mariah would be late and brought a magazine to read while he waited. Thirty minutes later, Mariah appeared.

"I'm so sorry I'm late. Hope you weren't waiting long." She opened the door and slid into the passenger seat.

"Just half an hour. We agreed eleven thirty." Emery put the car in gear and pulled away.

Mariah was defensive. "I can't help if I have a lot of patients to see."

Emery changed the subject and reopened the topic about applying aviation safety practices to medicine. Mariah listened with half her brain, not interested in aviation and not sure how this related to medicine. She pretended to understand what he was saying, but she couldn't imagine how a team-centered work environment could decrease medical errors or catastrophes like Penny's.

Emery realized he was losing Mariah's attention and commented instead on how nice the houses looked in David's neighborhood.

"Honey, can we look forward to something like this in the future?" Emery asked, pretending they were engaged.

Mariah imagined them together in a few years. "I hope so."

They turned onto David's street and parked on the side of the road across from his house, next to several other cars. Smoothing her skirt and blouse after sitting in the car, Mariah noticed Emery's attire. Red shorts, a yellow polo shirt, and loafers without socks—perfect for a picnic in suburban Philadelphia, but not for a christening party in Texas.

Mariah could not stop the words from popping out of her mouth. "Is that what you're wearing?" Once they were out, she couldn't help adding, "I thought you were going to wear khakis and a button-down shirt."

Emery's face fell. "Khakis would be too hot. Don't I look OK?"

"Well it's too late to go back now." Mariah pushed past him to the front door, hoping they could slip inside and find a quiet place out of sight.

David opened the door. A big smile came over his face as he announced to the group gathered in the living room, "Here comes the doctor who delivered Jared! Everyone! This is Mariah and her boyfriend..." He bent his head to Mariah's ear, quietly asking, "What's his name again?"

Mariah whispered, "Emery."

David announced to everyone grandly, "Mariah and Emery!" Then he turned to Mariah, eyeing Emery's shorts and loafers, "Do you two want some punch? All the food is in the kitchen, down the hallway and to the right."

"Thanks.." Mariah answered quickly. She wrapped her arm in Emery's and moved toward the kitchen, where a group of David's friends were helping themselves to hors d'oeuvres and punch.

Outfitted with a glass of punch and a snack, they let themselves out the back door of the kitchen onto a large porch. It was filled with Fisher-Price toys and a Little Tikes play kitchen. Beyond the porch, a huge swing set complete with a climbing wall filled most of the backyard.

This house was a kid's paradise.

"Hey! Wanna watch me dwive?" little Jane called to them as she sat in her pink Barbie car.

"Sure." Mariah said, trying to sound natural speaking to a three-year-old.

"He I go!"

The little girl propelled herself forward with her feet just like Fred Flintstone, scooting toward them with a grin made bigger by a red Kool-Aid stain that went halfway up her cheeks. She chugged along toward them and stopped at their feet, waiting for praise.

"That's very good, Jane," Mariah offered.

Jane smiled, turned her car around, and took off again. This time she went dangerously close to the top of the stairway that descended from the porch to the lawn.

"Hey! Don't go too far!" Mariah lunged toward the car, spilling her punch a little, just as Jane brought it to a stop.

Jane, adept at scaring adults with this little routine, began to laugh. "That's just what my Daddy says!"

"Cute kid." Emery took a sip of his punch and offered Mariah his napkin.

David's wife Joanne appeared, holding baby Jared. "There you are, Mariah. Want to see the baby you delivered three months ago?"

Mariah bounced Jared in her arms. "He's so big! I can't believe how much he's grown."

"He's fifteen pounds, five ounces!" Joanne announced triumphantly. "Why don't you two go in and join the party. Jane, Jared, and I will play out here for a little while."

The party was a success. Emery spent an hour talking to Todd Woods, who worked as a crop duster pilot before going to medical school. Mariah played croquet with her colleagues, read Jane a story, and held baby Jared whenever Joanne needed a break.

"I had a great time." Emery said as they drove home.

"Me too." Mariah smiled as she thought about David's kids. David's family life was harmonious despite the demands of his career.

Chapter Six

Laura awoke on Sunday morning with a migraine. She had to tell her mother that Penny and the baby were both dead. Laura planned to drive nonstop from Texas to Pennsylvania and tell her in person and she needed the hours behind the wheel to review her situation. Emery's rebuff annoyed her, but more than anything else, Laura feared telling her mother about Penny's death. Normally, Laura wouldn't care too much about her mother's feelings, but with Penny gone, she hoped to finally garner some of her mother's affection.

Laura was a victim of child abuse and had endured a traumatic childhood that left deep physical and emotional scars. She buried any weakness or vulnerability under a thick mantle of impenetrable confidence and trusted no one. The thought of driving twenty-six hours was disagreeable, but flying was definitely out of the question. She pulled her suitcase out from under her bed and threw in enough clothes for a long weekend.

Her mother, Amanda Reynolds, lived in government-subsidized housing outside Harrisburg. She had struggled with manic depression and addiction all her life. Jobs, relationships, medication, and money all seemed to pass uncontrollably through her tobacco-stained fingers. News of Penny's death could trigger a major reaction, or even suicide.

Penny was Amanda's favorite child, and Laura

had grown up in the shadow of affection meant for Penny. Laura had learned to deny her emotions and ignore the sting of her mother's indifference years ago, but deep inside there was still a little girl who wanted to be loved.

Penny's unplanned pregnancy didn't compromise Amanda's devotion. When Penny had announced she was pregnant four months ago, Amanda told Laura to look out for her younger sister and safeguard her care. Laura chose the best OB-GYN resident at BAMC to care for Penny, and Mariah let her down. Now that Penny was gone, Laura hoped to regain her mother's love. Planning to avenge Penny's death was a good first step.

As Laura drove through the night, memories from her childhood filled her mind. Amanda would sit at the kitchen table peeling an apple and waving the paring knife menacingly while Laura cooked dinner. Laura resembled her father, who abandoned their family a few weeks after she was born. Amanda couldn't stand to look at Laura across the dinner table. Once dinner was made, Laura ate by herself in her bedroom.

As the oldest daughter of an abusive, alcoholic mother, Laura learned to disappear the moment her mother became violent. Once that became impossible, Laura began sedating her mother with her own narcotic pills hidden in the wall behind the bathtub. A few crushed tablets mixed in her mother's drink ensured a quiet, safe evening for Laura and Penny. After some experience, Laura planted her mother's street drugs on the music teacher in middle school who embarrassed her in front of the class, and the boy who was expelled in high school after he teased her in biology.

The car's low fuel light chimed, and Laura's attention returned to the present. She pulled into a small gas station off a remote section of highway. A handsome, young man with greasy hands approached her car as she stepped out to pump the gas.

"There's no self-serve gasoline here, ma'am." He was polite and took the nozzle from her hands. Laura couldn't help noticing his broad shoulders and blond hair under the baseball cap.

"OK." She reluctantly released the nozzle. "Where's your restroom?"

"Out behind the station." He motioned with his head to a Porta-Potty shed standing slightly askew on a small berm behind the building. Laura tried to walk purposefully but tripped over the broken pavement, and once inside slammed the door loudly.

Cursing to herself as she made her way back, she chided, "You need a real restroom for your customers."

"That'll be twenty dollars, ma'am." The gas station attendant held out his greasy hand when she returned.

"Isn't windshield washing included with pumping gas anymore?" Laura frowned as she opened her wallet and handed him a twenty.

"No, ma'am. But if you'd like, I'll make an exception..." He turned to pick up the squeegee out of the bucket of dirty water. Laura fired up her car and sped off, narrowly missing his foot with her tire.

"No, thank you." Laura smiled to herself, watching the attendant fall backward in the rearview mirror. She felt vindicated.

Malignant intelligence was Laura's strongest asset. She delighted in tormenting people, especially her unwitting colleagues at work. Using a scheduling clerk's password, Laura randomly canceled her patients' appointments and double-booked other provider's schedules. Patients complained, and arguments between the staff could be heard in the waiting room. Everyone in the family practice clinic was unhappy except Laura.

When her clinic was slow, Laura checked the pharmacy logbook for familiar names. She read her coworkers' medical charts and spread rumors about their infections or other health problems. No one was safe from Laura.

Her actions went undetected until Monica Sims, a newly trained nurse practitioner, joined the family practice department. Monica uncovered Laura's scheduling changes, saw through her lies, and began to indict Laura for lateness, incomplete records, illegible writing, and poor teamwork in the clinic. Laura could no longer function just below the surface of scrutiny, and her prickly personality made her future with the clinic uncertain.

At first, Laura didn't mind Monica's meddling; she had fulfilled her military obligation and planned to leave the clinic at the end of the summer anyway. Tired of listening to sick patients' complaints, Laura wanted a job that didn't involve any patient care. A vaccine research facility in Atlanta needed a nurse practitioner to help organize clinical trials. The job required tracking patients with advanced cervical cancer who were given an experimental HPV 16 vaccine—mostly paperwork and follow-up phone calls. This seemed perfect until Penny announced she was pregnant and Amanda demanded Laura supervise her OB care.

Suddenly, Laura needed to retain her family practice position for the duration of Penny's pregnancy, and Monica's interference became her only obstacle. Resorting to her old methods, Laura spiked Monica's coffee with powder from Percocet capsules on the morning of the military's routine drug testing. Monica tested positive for narcotics and was gone within a week.

Now that Penny was dead, Laura hoped the job in Atlanta was still available. Wasn't Mariah Gordon also moving to Georgia? Laura concentrated on a plan for revenge as she drove the final few hours toward Harrisburg.

Laura grew up in a rundown rented farmhouse outside of West Philadelphia. She remembered coming home each day after school hoping to find her mother dead on the floor. Five years ago, after a prolonged admission to rehab, Amanda moved to a government-subsidized apartment on the outskirts of Harrisburg. Laura didn't miss the farmhouse but wondered how her mother could find her apartment among the rows of identical buildings.

Amanda, wearing a dirty housecoat, opened the door of her apartment. "What are you doing here?"

Judging by her disheveled hair and the mess in the apartment, Laura could tell Amanda wasn't doing well. There was no point in small talk with this woman; Laura needed to inform Amanda of Penny's death right away

Walking past her mother, Laura was overcome by the smell of stale cigarettes and urine. "Don't worry, Mom, I didn't drive all the way from Texas to visit you. I have important news. Sit down." Laura pushed a pile of magazines and newspapers off the couch and motioned for her mother to sit.

"What is it? How is Penny? Why didn't she come with you?" Amanda worked hard to stay coherent.

"Penny is dead." Laura stated. "She was in a car accident; her baby died, and then she died, too."

Amanda stared blankly for a moment and then demanded, "What are you telling me? Penny is dead? How can she be dead? You were supposed to be watching out for her." She grabbed Laura's arm and shook her.

Laura briefly flashed back to her childhood. She looked around at her mother's filthy apartment, and the reality of the situation returned. Why did she want to be loved by this sick, depraved old woman? It was irrational, but she still wanted her approval. Laura stood up and faced her mother, hoping she was lucid enough to understand. "Penny is dead, and I'm going to get even with the doctor who let her die."

For the first time in thirty years, Amanda Reynolds smiled at Laura.

Chapter Seven

A week later, Mariah cornered David as he was leaving his office. "Do you think there was anything more I could have done to save Penny?"

David put his briefcase back on his desk and sat down. "Mariah, you were there at the interdepartmental review. The members of Risk Management found there was nothing that could have been done to save Penny. From the moment she was in the car accident, she was destined to have the placental abruption that would kill her baby and then her. If you had monitored that baby, which was previable, and therefore not normal practice, you might have noticed when the abruption occurred, but you still would not have acted differently until you discovered she was developing DIC. You might have checked labs sooner and been a little ahead of the curve as she began to decompensate. In the end, a C-section would have been the last resort and not performed until her DIC was already threatening her life. The outcome was inevitable when the car hit the guardrail, and there's nothing we could do to change that."

Mariah shook her head as she sat in the chair across from his desk. "It just seems unbelievable that she died. I feel I'm to blame. I think that if I had tried harder and gone to the ER earlier, maybe this would not have happened."

David smiled. "That's because you're a good

doctor and you care about your patients. But even the best doctors can't save every patient. Sometimes young, healthy patients die despite our best efforts, and everyone has trouble accepting this fact. People, especially loved ones, want to blame someone for their loss. Often the doctor, rightly or wrongly, is in the crosshairs. Mariah, you can try to work harder and be more conscientious, but that will not change what has happened. You are a good doctor; you just need to believe in yourself and have the confidence to do what is right."

"Thanks," she said weakly. She needed that pep talk. She was on call again tonight.

Emery was back home in Philadelphia when Mariah called.

"Hello." he said, and added quickly, "Ow! Shit!"

Mariah heard the commotion. "Are you all right? What's going on?"

"I'm OK, I just burned myself on the oven. Wow that hurts! Any idea what to do for a burn?"

At least I can give one piece of medical advice, Mariah thought to herself. "Hold your hand under cold running water, and it will feel better. Then cover it with a dry bandage." Mariah could hear water running in the kitchen sink a second later.

Emery sighed, "That's much better. How's it going, hon? Still bummed out about the patient you lost?"

Emery's trivialization of her emotions made Mariah mad, and she lashed out. "I'm not bummed out.

I'm just trying to call you to see how you're doing. If you don't want to talk, I can call back later." Mariah started to put the receiver down.

Emery pleaded, "No! Don't hang up. Why don't you pour yourself a drink and tell me what's going on."

"I don't need a drink. I'm on call and going for a run. I'll call you back later." Mariah hung up.

Labor and delivery was quiet, Mariah had time for a quick run. Quickly changing into sneakers, a T-shirt, and shorts, Mariah grabbed her beeper and ran down the back stairs and out into the hot evening air. The sun was low, and the streets of Fort Sam Houston were lined with old, live oak trees, shading most of her two-mile loop. Her beeper went off at the halfway mark, and labor and delivery's number flashed.

Complaining loudly, she ran back. The tranquility of running along the old avenues faded as she approached the hospital.

Bernice bustled past a sweaty, panting Mariah. "Bonnie Thompson, the widow with the kids injured in the plane crash, is in labor." She held an IV in one hand and a syringe of Nubaine painkiller in the other.

That afternoon, when Bonnie began contracting, she called her mother-in-law. They had planned for this moment; Betty was in charge of her kids, and Ralph, her father-in-law, drove Bonnie to the hospital. By the time she arrived at BAMC she was six centimeters dilated, wanted an epidural for pain control, and still wondered how she could deliver her baby without her husband.

She became more upset as her labor progressed. She started to ask, "Is there any way I can have a C-section now?"

Mariah checked her cervix; she was nine centimeters. She touched Bonnie's shoulder and smiled calmly. "It's almost time to push! Let's get you into the delivery room, and you'll have this baby in your arms before we could do a C-section."

Bonnie was scared, and so was Ralph. He was completely unprepared to be a labor coach. When it came time to deliver, he disappeared.

Mariah and Bernice coached Bonnie together. "You can do this! You're almost there, and the baby is doing great!"

Bernice was soothing and encouraging. "Honey, your husband would be so proud of you! I can see him looking down from Heaven. He's smiling because he's so happy you are bringing his baby into the world naturally."

Bonnie put her faith in Bernice and Mariah, and together they worked and pushed until she delivered a beautiful, healthy baby girl. The scene in the delivery room was bittersweet. Bonnie cried for joy and grieved that her husband was not present as she brought their third child into the world.

While Bonnie recovered in the delivery room, Ralph reappeared at her side.

"I'm sorry I panicked, Bonnie." He looked at the

doorway to the delivery room. "I called Betty and asked her to come right away, and she brought the kids. Now that the baby's here, I know Kyle would like to see you. I'll stay with Betty and Kaylie in the waiting room."

As Kyle entered the delivery room, he looked overwhelmed seeing his mom holding the baby and wasn't really sure how to act. As Bonnie nursed his baby sister, he seemed happy to be part of it.

Mariah smiled as she left Bonnie alone with her son and new baby. Moments like this reminded her why she loved being a doctor.

Chapter Eight

Laura pulled into BAMC's parking lot for the last time. Texan sunshine briefly blinded her as she put on her green army cap and replaced her sunglasses. Today was Laura's first and last day back to work after Penny's death. Having fulfilled her army commitment, Laura combined her bereavement and terminal leave, which gave her ample time to interview and accept her new job in Atlanta. She planned to clean out her desk and then track down Mariah Gordon.

The family practice clinic was busy. Ten doctors and four nurse practitioners were seeing patients; the waiting room was packed to standing room only. A TV droned CNN, and everyone stared vacantly at the screen or blankly ahead. Children whimpered softly in their mothers' laps, and babies occasionally cried. Laura enjoyed walking through the waiting room knowing that none of these patients were scheduled to see her.

A new nurse practitioner sat at Laura's old desk, talking on the phone. She nodded her head toward Laura's stuff, packed into boxes and stacked in the corner of the office. She whispered to Laura while still on the phone, "I hope you don't mind, but I put your things in boxes so I could move in to your office."

Laura scowled, picked up a box, and went in search of an unoccupied wheelchair. Laura stacked her boxes on the wheelchair's vinyl seat and pushed them down the hall to the elevator. Quickly loading the boxes in her car, Laura left the wheelchair in the parking lot. It was time to find Mariah.

The OB clinic receptionist told Laura that Mariah was working on labor and delivery. Laura hit the elevator button for the fifth floor and waited. Unlike most people, Laura thrived on conflict and confrontation; she smiled with anticipation. Mariah was responsible for Penny's death, and Laura wanted her to pay dearly. Mariah would never know what hit her.

Earlier that day, Mariah heard Laura was back. Nervous about seeing her again, she asked the labor and delivery nurses for help managing a confrontation with Laura. They agreed the best strategy was to be boldly sympathetic and overtly friendly; this would catch Laura off guard. Mariah hoped using positive words to overcome the negative would avoid a torrent of sharp comments and name-calling altogether.

In anticipation of the showdown, the labor and delivery clerk called the OB clinic clerk and asked to be notified when Laura was on her way up. They got the call and the nurses' station was buzzing with anticipation.

Laura walked out of the elevator on the fifth floor. Labor and delivery was down the hall on the right. Two laboring women occasionally yelled or cried out, but their agony didn't distract her. She was intent on finding Mariah.

Stopping a nurse, she asked, "Where is Dr.

Gordon?" Looking past the nurse, she saw Mariah sitting in the nurses' station.

Seeing Laura, Mariah hurried over and greeted her warmly. "Hi, Laura! I'm so glad to see you. How are you?" Laura stiffened as Mariah gave her an awkward hug and continued, "Is there anything I can do?"

The nurses' station became silent as everyone strained to hear the conversation.

Mariah continued, "As a result of Penny's tragedy, I'm presenting a policy to the hospital administration mandating that all OB patients are monitored in the ER if they are observed for thirty minutes or more. That should remind everyone that all pregnant patients are actually *two* patients, and ignoring that second patient in their belly is a perilous mistake."

Letting Mariah prattle about the ER gave Laura a moment to calculate her comeback. "I think that's the least you could do. What about ensuring that the patients are seen by an OB doc right away, not four hours later?"

Mariah was prepared for Laura's question. "That's part of the policy." Changing the subject, Mariah added, "I heard that today is your last day and you're going to head a research project in Atlanta!"

Laura couldn't resist boasting. "Yes, I'll be the new patient liaison for a cervical cancer vaccine trial."

Mariah seemed genuinely interested. "Is that the HPV virus vaccine? I've heard promising things about the preliminary studies."

Laura realized that Mariah's small talk was

leading her away from the purpose of her visit. It was time to take control. "Yes, it's in preliminary trials, vaccinating women who already have cervical cancer and then following them prospectively. But I didn't come here to talk about my new job, Mariah."

Laura's eyes narrowed and her hands moved to her hips. "Why did it take you so long to see Penny in the ER?"

Mariah answered by evading the question. "Laura, we did our best to save Penny, but the moment her car hit the guardrail, her life was over."

Laura coolly replied, "Maybe your best isn't good enough. If you'd seen her in the ER, she'd still be alive today, and her baby, too."

Mariah repeated, "I'm sorry, Laura. We did everything possible to save her,"

Laura persisted. "If you were a better doctor, she'd still be alive."

Mariah's expression froze as if Laura had struck a chord.

Laura sensed Mariah's vulnerability and pushed harder. "You could've saved her if you tried harder, knew more, and were better prepared. Dr. Blackstone has more experience with critical patients. I'm sure if she'd been on call, Penny would still be alive." Laura knew she'd played a winning card.

The elevator doors opened and Jenna Blackstone stepped out. Tracy had paged Jenna to labor and delivery stat when Laura had arrived, hoping she could intervene on Mariah's behalf. Mariah passed her without a word, wiping her eyes and hurrying toward the resident locker room. Jenna realized she was a few moments too late and jogged down the hall after Mariah.

"Hey, Mariah...Dr. Gordon!" Jenna called as she followed her down the hall. A few patients were in the hall, and everyone was staring as Mariah closed the locker room door behind her. Jenna pulled it open and went in.

"I'm sorry Laura got to you like that." Jenna reached out and touched Mariah's shoulder.

"What if she's right?" Mariah couldn't help letting the words out even though Jenna had not heard the conversation.

"She's not right, and you know it. And if you don't, you should." Jenna guessed at what Laura must have said to make Mariah so upset.

She moistened a face cloth from the bathroom sink for Mariah. "Here, wipe your face and get that mascara off your cheeks. Don't let that bitch get to you. I don't know why you agreed to deliver her sister anyway." Jenna was doing her best to be supportive, but her real strength was fighting. "If she talks to you again, just call me, and I promise I will take her out."

Mariah blew her nose and wiped mascara off her cheeks. "She's leaving. And in two weeks, so are we. Thank God for that." She looked Jenna in the eye. "Do I look like I've been crying?" Mariah's bloodshot eyes and blotchy face cracked into a pathetic smile.

Jenna nodded, opened her locker, and took out her purse. "I don't have much in here, but this should help." She brushed blush powder all over Mariah's face to even out the blotches. "There, now you look like you were in the sun too long."

"Like that could ever happen." Mariah took a quick look in the mirror. "Thanks. You want to get a beer after work? You're not on call, are you?"

"Sorry, kid. I switched with Kirsten. Maybe we can make it another time when we're both free?"

"That sounds good. Thanks for being there for me." Mariah left the locker room and walked past the nurses' station with her head held high; it wasn't the first time they'd seen a resident cry at work.

Chapter Nine

The final day of residency ended without ceremony. The sun was setting behind the apartment building as Mariah parked Irving; the shade cooled the air. Acknowledging the completion of an epic chapter in her life, she rested her head against the steering wheel. Mariah felt proud and fulfilled by her accomplishment—and a little uneasy about her next assignment. She looked up to see Emery illuminated in the kitchen window, placing a pan in the oven. He had flown in earlier that day to attend the graduation dinner.

God love him! Mariah thought as she got out of the car, picked up her briefcase, and took her on-call bag out of the trunk. She was famished and felt the weight of the day falling away as she climbed the stairs to the front door. Her keys were in her purse, and her hands were full. She tried to tap the door lightly with her foot but it sounded more like kicking the door down. A minute later, Emery, flushed from the heat of the oven and wearing her floral apron smeared with barbeque sauce, opened the door.

"Are you *kicking* the door after I slaved to cook us dinner?" Emery's smile belied his words.

Mariah stepped inside and fell into his embrace. "My arms were full and I couldn't get my keys out of my purse," she pretended to whine, and kissed him.

"Never mind. Go get changed out of that sexy uniform. I made us a delicious dinner, and I'm starving."

Mariah left the room, trailing clothes seductively as she walked to the bedroom. Tossing off her black high heels and unwinding her hair always felt wonderful, especially when she didn't have to work the next day. Mariah was tempted to lie down on the bed and have a quick snooze. But that would be the end of the night, and Emery had worked so hard on dinner. Instead, she put on gym shorts and a gray "ARMY" T-shirt and walked back into the kitchen.

"Want a beer?" Mariah grabbed two beers from the refrigerator and offered Emery one.

"Thanks. Have you ever tried popovers?" He took a big swig of his beer. Smoke started billowing from the oven, and the smell was not appetizing. Unfazed, Emery reached an oven-mitted hand into the smoke and brought out a muffin pan full of dark-brown, crispy popovers. He beamed as if they were a culinary triumph.

Mariah sipped her beer and noticed how cute he looked in her apron. "All this work. When did you get in?" Mariah grabbed a dishtowel and began to fan the smoke alarm.

Emery placed two popovers on each plate and ladled barbequed pork over his and creamy vegetables over Mariah's. "I arrived about an hour ago and had the taxi stop at Bill Miller's Barbeque. The barbeque and veggies both looked so good I got them to go, and popovers only take a minute once the oven heats up."

Mariah threw the dishtowel at Emery. "Fan the smoke detector. I'll open more windows." After a few minutes of fanning, the smoke cleared enough for them to sit down to dinner.

Emery asked cautiously, "How was your last day of residency?"

"It went well. A very full day." Mariah tried not to talk while chewing. "I transferred all my patients to the third-year resident. It feels great to be done."

Mariah ticked off a list of events in her mind. "The graduation ceremony is tomorrow at two, and dinner with the whole department is at six. We'll have to pack tomorrow morning, and the movers will come the day after graduation. Then we're on vacation for two whole weeks." Mariah smiled and took another swig of beer.

It was going to be a very busy two weeks, without much time for fun, but Mariah had not had two weeks off since medical school. They planned to drive Irving to Pennsylvania, pack Emery's things into his car, and drive to Fort Benning. Columbus was the town adjacent to Fort Benning, where Mariah rented them an apartment. If all went according to plan, they would move Emery's boxes into their new apartment the day before Mariah's boxes arrived.

"How was your last day at the law firm?" Mariah reached across the table and touched Emery's hand.

"Good. One of the partners stopped by to say good-bye. He's the one who helped me get the job in Atlanta. He said I could always come back if things didn't work out or I didn't pass the Georgia bar..." Emery smiled and took a swig of beer. Quitting his job to move in with Mariah was a big commitment; he hoped there would be no regrets.

Four years ago, while still in law school, Emery had decided that Mariah was the only woman for him, and once, during a moment of tenderness, he told her that he wanted to marry her. "Whenever you're ready, just ask me and I'll accept," was how he had proposed.

Since then, the ups and downs of their long-distance relationship were a challenge. Emery stayed committed to Mariah throughout her difficult residency in Texas because he believed they had a bright future together. Emery felt sure their relationship would flourish once Mariah completed residency and began working more regular hours as a staff physician.

"Is everything OK?" Emery looked down at Mariah's hand.

"Of course, can't I hold your hand?" She smiled.

"Sure, you just don't usually make much contact during dinner." Emery continued to eat with one hand.

"I was thinking about our future living situation. You know, in Georgia, when we move in together."

"Are you having second thoughts?" He slowly put his fork full of food down on the plate. He could never count on Mariah's responses when it came to talking about their relationship. Her family experiences scared her away from serious relationships, and just trying to get her to agree to live together involved an eternal discussion of pros and cons.

"No. I guess I just wanted to make it more official. I think that if we move to Georgia together, it's a sign that we are committing ourselves to this relationship and to each other. I think it warrants substantiation."

"You mean get married?" Emery practically vaulted over the table to give Mariah a hug. He knew this was her strange way of committing herself to him. Emery picked Mariah up in his arms and sat down in her chair. Holding her in his lap, her small frame comfortably folded under his clasped hands. He smiled and kissed her tenderly.

Mariah looked at Emery. "Does this mean you want to have sex now, because I'm still pretty hungry," she asked.

"I don't want to have sex right now. I mean, I do, but I can wait ten or twenty minutes. This is a big decision for you and a big step for us."

For a moment, the enormity of the decision unnerved Mariah. The rest of her life was a long time. *What if it doesn't work out?* Mariah's face looked worried and almost sad.

Oblivious, Emery continued, "I can't believe we're engaged." Adding, "Especially since my parents just called today and asked if we were going to visit before moving to Georgia."

Mariah's face fell. Emery's parents didn't seem to approve of their relationship and she barely knew them.

"Relax. I told them we could only stay for one night," Emery soothed Mariah.

"OK. That'll be great," she said halfheartedly.

"Yes." Emery smiled and continued. "We'll tell them about our engagement when we visit. What about a ring?" Now Emery's face became serious. "I need to get you a ring."

"Don't worry about it." Wedding protocols didn't interest Mariah. "A ring is just a small token of our commitment to each other."

"Yes. That's why I want it to be special." He smiled again. "Do you have any preferences?"

Mariah ate another bite and said, "No." Then she changed her mind. "Actually, something small that won't catch on exam gloves. I must be able to remove it quickly when I deliver a baby or go into surgery. I can't wear any rings on my hands when I scrub."

Mariah added, "Let's not set a wedding date yet, OK? I want to get through the move and start my new job before planning a wedding."

"OK," Emery agreed in a voice that was serious and matter-of-fact.

"Good." Mariah picked up her plate and headed toward the dishwasher. She smiled and looked over her shoulder. "Hasn't it been ten or twenty minutes?"

Chapter Ten

After a long and arduous four-year residency, graduation was remarkably understated. The chief residents and attending doctors wore dress-green uniforms and assembled in the Morning Report conference room. Certificates were handed out, along with awards for special accomplishments. Mariah received the American Association of Gynecologic Laparoscopy's Award for her skill in laparoscopy, and Jenna received the Best Gynecologic Surgeon Award. Four years of sacrifice and hard work were commemorated with a thirty-minute ceremony and a group photo.

Graduation dinner, as a tradition, was conducted as a military "dining out" with spouses and dates at a restaurant on San Antonio's River Walk. It was a formal dinner with some basic rules and military traditions. A junior officer nicknamed "Mr. Vice" emceed the evening and proposed the first of many serious and humorous toasts. The residents supplied a large bowl of strong punch and a few gag gifts to make the evening fun.

Everyone dressed in his or her best civilian clothes, and fashion took a holiday. Accustomed to wearing a uniform almost every day, most of attending doctors had donated their unused civilian clothes to the poor.

Once a year, they resignedly squeezed into one of their few remaining civilian outfits for the graduation dinner. Dr. Halligan dusted off his light-green leisure suit, and everyone joked that he just couldn't get enough green polyester. Dr. Nelson and his wife made a cute couple; his pink button-down shirt matched her pink dress, and they both wore white shoes. David's multicolored cowboy boots flashed beneath dry-cleaned blue jeans that still had a crease down the front. Joanna, his "cowgirl" wife, wore matching boots with a leather vest and jean skirt.

A few of the graduating residents committed their own fashion faux pas. Sam Michaels had a fetish for gaudy turquoise bolo ties, and Kirsten Smith wore a dress that was too short and too frilly. Jenna Blackstone couldn't help rolling her eyes at Mariah when she saw Kirsten arrive. Jenna's knee-length black skirt and blue silk blouse looked very conservative compared to her husband, Floyd's, Tommy Bahama Hawaiian shirt and khaki shorts. Mariah wore a simple black sheath dress with a gold necklace, and Emery looked comfortable in his camel khakis and polo shirt.

Sam was "Mr. Vice" and asked everyone to be seated. The waiters and waitresses passed champagne to everyone for a toast, and Sam invited Dr. Chickweir to speak first.

Raising his glass of champagne, Dr. Chickweir began his toast. "You're well-trained doctors and have no reason to worry about your next assignment. But let me warn you, it's different practicing medicine on your own." Dr. Chickweir paused and looked around the room. "There aren't any attending doctors to sign off on your decisions.

You are completely responsible for all the decisions you make. And to remind you of that fact," he said, pulling a bag out from under his chair, "we are giving each of you a yo-yo. Not because you'll have time to play at your new assignment, but because yo-yo stands for 'you're on your own.'" He raised his glass to the group and took a sip.

Everyone laughed and chimed in, "Hear! Hear!" The champagne bubbles stung Mariah's nose.

Sam continued from the podium, "Dr. Gordon will now present the first award."

Rubbing her nose briefly, Mariah held her glass up. "Dr. Nelson, we would like to thank you for your leadership and unfailing faith in us—no matter how badly we screwed up. We appreciated hearing your fair and often positive opinions about our work in Morning Report. Unfortunately, your voice was often drowned out by Dr. Halligan's louder and less positive comments." Mariah leaned over and retrieved a large bullhorn from a bag she'd smuggled in earlier. "The next time you have a positive opinion to express in Morning Report and find your voice is not being heard, simply press this button and"—Mariah held the bullhorn in front of her face— "LET EVERYONE KNOW YOU WANT TO BE HEARD." Everyone chuckled, and Mariah sat down, happy to have completed her part in the dining out.

Jenna was next. "Dr. Halligan, we know you breed Great Danes and are familiar with this special instrument." Jenna held a silver dog whistle up for everyone to see. "For those of you who are unfamiliar, this is a dog whistle.

It produces a sound that only dogs can hear. For your convenience, Dr. Halligan, we implanted a special receiver in each new chief resident's ear. When you want a resident to come, blow this silent whistle, and they will appear!"

Kirsten's turn was next. "Ultrasound has become an important diagnostic tool for both obstetrics and reproductive endocrinology. Dr. Chamberlain's and Dr. Chickweir's patients often look at the images on the machine with confusion. These removable stickers with sayings like 'Hi, Mom' or 'That IS what you think it is!' can be applied to the display screen to enhance your patient's understanding and ultrasound experience."

Sam was last to toast and addressed the group with his glass held high. "As you all know, Dr. Mettson is leaving BAMC to join Walter Reed's Gynecologic Oncology Department. As graduating residents, we'd be much more sad if we weren't leaving ourselves! We heard it's almost impossible to drive around DC without getting lost. As a going-away gift, we got you a road map of downtown Washington, DC."

Everyone chuckled. "Hear! Hear!"

Dinner arrived, and the room hummed with conversation, jokes, and laughter.

As the evening drew to a close, Dr. Halligan stood up with his glass in hand. "I'm really going to miss you kids, especially Kirsten's dance steps on the desktop. But seriously, you're a damn good group of doctors. I'm damn proud of y'all." Dr. Halligan lifted his glass for a toast.

The attending doctors all stood and toasted the graduating residents. "Hear! Hear!" The graduation party ended. They were on their own.

Chapter Eleven

Fort Benning, known as the "Home of the Infantry," trained and supported over one hundred thousand active duty infantry soldiers, dependents, and retirees. The Infantry School and airborne training towers inspired patriotism and respect for the soldiers' daring commitment and sacrifice. Mariah was proud to be serving at Fort Benning again.

Joining the US Army had not been Mariah's plan after high school, but college tuition was expensive. ROTC offered her a full scholarship, and she was intrigued by the idea of serving her country in the military.

Mariah had wanted to give something back to her country. As a high school exchange student in Normandy, France, she experienced the life of a European citizen. As a result, Mariah developed a new appreciation for the freedoms and opportunities she enjoyed as an American citizen. Her tour inspired a desire to serve her country in return for these benefits.

Mariah's pride in America grew while living in Normandy. Remnants of World War II were still visible everywhere, especially on the beaches. The American soldiers' bravery and sacrifice were undeniable as she stared at the cliffs above the beaches they scaled on D-Day. The residents of Bayeux still appreciated being liberated in World War II, and remembered the American soldiers' sacrifice. Mariah felt an obligation to give something back to her country that gave her and others so much.

The US Army wanted intelligent, athletic college students to mold into officers and offered eligible candidates a full scholarship in return for four years of service. Mariah signed the paperwork, passed the physical, and accepted the commitment before telling her parents.

ROTC's leadership training and opportunities changed Mariah's life. She earned "airborne wings" at Fort Benning's paratrooper school and became a student battalion commander senior year. Her experiences in ROTC and at Fort Benning during college gave her self-confidence to apply and excel in medical school.

As Mariah drove onto Fort Benning, Monday, July 5, 1999, she was surprised at how different everything looked; the track and training fields looked smaller and were miles away from the hospital. She barely recognized the barracks where she had stayed during airborne training. However, the nearby strip malls full of bars, adult video stores, and tattoo parlors were unchanged. Fort Benning still exuded the familiar "high and tight" military character charged with adrenaline and testosterone.

Every female soldier, dependent wife, and dependent daughter stationed at Fort Benning was eligible for health care at Mitchel Army Community Hospital (MACH). As a result, MACH's labor and delivery was full of laboring women, and the OB-GYN clinic was routinely overbooked. Gynecology appointments were scheduled four to eight weeks in advance, and the pile of tubal ligation request forms was over six inches high; some requests were more than two years old.

The department had been running short-staffed for a year. Dr. Morales, chief of the department, was sick with kidney stones and frequently canceled his clinic and call duties. Dr. Kenneth Samuelson and Dr. Jane Kennedy were assisted by two civilian partners: Dr. Parsons, an ob-gyn in Columbus who took call on Wednesday nights and Saturdays, and Dr. Gottlieb, who saw GYN clinic patients and performed GYN surgery. In addition, a nurse practitioner, Helen DeVaney, also saw OB-GYN patients in the clinic.

Dr. Samuelson introduced Mariah to the staff in the OB-GYN clinic and on labor and delivery, and then took her for a brief tour of the hospital. Mariah smiled and struggled to remember everyone's names as she shook about thirty hands.

Dr. Samuelson and Dr. Kennedy were relieved to have Mariah join their staff and finally get some help. Ken was married with two small children whom he barely knew, and Jane's marriage was ending in divorce. She didn't smile much, but she was very happy to meet Mariah.

The family practice doctors also cared for a small percentage of OB patients and did a few deliveries. MACH had a family practice residency program, and their residents rotated through most of the departments in the hospital. Teaching residents was challenging when the patient load was high, but Mariah was excited.

By 9:00 a.m., Mariah was busy on labor and delivery, completing a history and physical for a young woman in labor with her first child. The patient was healthy, her pregnancy was uncomplicated, and Mariah smiled to herself as she finished the admission orders. Today was her first day as a staff physician. She thought about Dr. Chickweir's yo-yo. No longer insulated by an attending doctor, she was solely responsible for her actions, orders, procedures, and medical decisions.

MACH's labor and delivery rooms each had state-of-the-art computerized fetal heart monitoring. Display monitors continually traced a bright orange line against a dark background for each pregnant woman in labor or undergoing evaluation. At this moment, each of the jagged and irregular patterns fell within the highlighted safety margins and indicated fetal well-being. Computerized fetal monitoring was new technology for Mariah, but she quickly learned to navigate the system and appreciated the ability to monitor all the laboring patients' tracings from the nurses' station instead of going to each patient's bedside to inspect paper tracings.

The nurses were nice and made an effort to get to know Mariah as they worked together. This labor and delivery was busier than BAMC, but the cases were low risk and less complex. Any stable, high-risk OB patient was transferred to the County Medical Center in Columbus or to Eisenhower Army Medical Center near Augusta.

A call came in from the ER as Mariah sat watching the labor monitor, and the unit clerk handed her the phone.

"Dr. Gordon here," Mariah spoke as she put the phone to her ear.

"Are you the new ob-gyn?" The ER doctor's southern accent rolled into her ear, calming her slight apprehension. He sounded friendly.

"Yes. I just started today."

"Well, I'm Dr. Peter Kline, and I have a patient with an ectopic pregnancy here for you," he drawled.

An ectopic pregnancy was a potential emergency, but Mariah was savvy to ER doctors trying to "dump" any female patient aged sixteen to fifty with abdominal pain and a positive pregnancy test on the ob-gyn on call. She quickly asked for clarification. "How do you know she has an ectopic? Did she have an ultrasound?"

"Yes. She had an ultrasound three days ago that read, 'Fetal cardiac motion outside of uterus — probable ectopic pregnancy.' Now she's having lots of pain and looks very pale. I have a blood count pending, want me to get a type and cross match?" Dr. Kline was nearing the limit of his patience.

"Yes. I'll be right down. Sounds like she needs to go to the OR. Don't let her eat or drink anything." Mariah's heart was pumping. She was thinking about surgery as she took the stairs down to the ER. What kind of laparoscopy equipment did this OR have? Was the patient stable? Would she operate alone, or would one of her new colleagues assist her?

Mariah entered the ER and identified Dr. Kline. He was an enormous man.

Carrying two ER charts and obviously in a hurry, he greeted her with a hearty handshake. "Welcome to Mitchell Army Community Hospital! Your patient is in room three. I started two large-bore IVs and ordered two units of blood cross matched for her, just in case." He winked in a lighthearted attempt to acknowledge the risk of catastrophic hemorrhage inherent with an ectopic pregnancy.

Mariah picked up the chart for room three and quickly skimmed the patient's medical history. She read the ultrasound report: "Diagnosis—Probable Ectopic Pregnancy." It was dated three days ago.

A very pale black female lay in the fetal position on the ER exam table. Captain Roberta Stevens was in a lot of pain.

The chart showed her pulse was ninety-five—too fast for a young, athletic female officer. Mariah suspected that the ectopic pregnancy had already ruptured and she was bleeding internally.

"Hello, Captain Stevens. My name is Dr. Gordon, and I'm an ob-gyn. Dr. Kline asked me to see you because you're having worsening pain and the ultrasound report I have here from Friday confirms you have an ectopic pregnancy. That means your pregnancy is not in your womb. It's rupturing your fallopian tube, making you bleed inside your abdomen. That's why you are having such severe pain."

Captain Stevens pushed up on her elbows. "I've been trying to get pregnant for two years. Is there any way you can move the pregnancy into my womb?"

Mariah was firm. "No, I can't. I'm very sorry. But we have to operate right away to remove the pregnancy and stop the bleeding, or you could be in danger of dying."

Captain Stevens's eyes narrowed. "You're going to take my baby out of me? Won't that kill her?"

Mariah replied a little too coldly, "This pregnancy was never going to grow into a baby. Since you are bleeding inside your abdomen, it has likely already died."

Captain Stevens shook her head. "My baby's dead?"

Seeing her patient's reaction, Mariah began again, "Captain Stevens, I appreciate how much you wanted this pregnancy, and if I could move it into your womb, I would in a heartbeat. But research has shown us that ectopic pregnancies are often not normal, that's probably why they implanted in the fallopian tube. Saving an abnormal pregnancy isn't what you want. What we need to do is get this situation resolved so you can get pregnant again." Mariah tried to finish on an upbeat image of the future.

Captain Stevens's face fell as she realized her pregnancy was over and surgery was necessary to keep her healthy enough to get pregnant again. She accepted the plan but wanted to know if her boyfriend could be present for the operation. Mariah explained that her significant other could see her before the surgery if he arrived very soon.

Mariah found the ER clerk and asked, "Where do you keep your surgical paperwork packets? And what's the phone extension for the OR?" The din of activity in the ER made it hard to be heard.

"Here's an OR packet, and I already gave them a heads up that you would be calling them." She smiled until her headset rang again.

Mariah was surprised by the upbeat attitude of everyone in this busy ER. The clerks were never this helpful in residency. She dialed the OR and held for the anesthesia doctor on call.

"This is Dr. Lamont."

"Hi. This is Dr. Gordon. I have a thirty-year-old active duty patient with an ectopic pregnancy. I think she's already ruptured and bleeding internally. She needs to get into the OR stat."

"OK, send her right up. I'll get a room ready."

"I will, thanks. Oh and can you please tell me how I get to the OR from the ER? This is my first day, and my tour did not cover that!" After a second of silence, Mariah realized she was holding a dead line.

Mariah finished the preoperative paperwork quickly and went to find the OR. Captain Stevens's boyfriend had already arrived, and she was on her way up to the OR. A quick phone call to labor and delivery confirmed no one was likely to deliver or need a doctor while Mariah operated.

The surgery went smoothly, and Mariah was able to save Captain Stevens's fallopian tube. After completing paperwork and dictation, Mariah headed back up to labor and delivery. The moment she sat down, the ER called her again.

"Hello again!" Dr. Kline's southern drawl reminded Mariah of his enormous shape, holding charts and bowling around the crowded ER.

"Hello, Dr. Kline. What is it now?" Mariah wanted to be nice but not a pushover. She didn't want him to call her for every small gynecologic problem that came to the ER.

"There's a patient here with vaginal bleeding and an infection after a hysterectomy. I gave her antibiotics and fluids, but her white count is high, and she vomits anything she drinks. I can't send her home like this."

"OK, I just finished in the OR and have to check on my patients on labor and delivery. I'll be there in a little while." Mariah sighed. Being pulled from one place to another was hard; she hated leaving labor and delivery unsupervised for long periods of time.

One labor patient was doing well and would soon begin pushing. The other patient's labor had stopped progressing

This required an evaluation of her labor. Were the contractions strong enough? Was the baby too big? Was the birth canal too small? And how was the baby tolerating labor? Mariah's evaluation revealed the patient's contractions were not strong or frequent enough. Weak contractions are made stronger by giving the patient Pitocin. Once all the orders and notes were written, Mariah descended the back stairs to the ER. Her patient was again waiting in room three, but this scenario was totally different.

Rose Bouton sat on the exam table. Her sister and ten-year-old daughter sat next to her, looking very distraught. Olive-skinned and slightly overweight, Rose looked Mediterranean. Her daughter, Emily, had Rose's skin and features. This sad, quiet child appeared accustomed to waiting for hours with her mother.

Mariah greeted the group. "I'm Dr. Gordon. Sorry you had to wait, I was finishing a surgery. When did you start feeling poorly, Mrs. Bouton?"

"She never felt well again after the hysterectomy!" her sister blurted out. Mariah couldn't tell if she was distressed about her sister's illness or angry about her prior medical care.

Mariah spoke to Rose. "I don't have any records of your surgery in this chart. When and where did you have the hysterectomy?"

"Two weeks ago at the county hospital in Columbus. I have cervical cancer, and they did a radical hysterectomy. But they said they didn't get it all, and now I might need radiation."

"Oh," Mariah said. This didn't imply a good prognosis for Rose. Rose had metastatic cervical cancer. It had spread beyond her cervix and uterus. She needed radiation to kill the cancer cells left after surgery.

Today, Rose had pain and a fever likely from decay of cancerous tissues left behind after her hysterectomy. The exam confirmed Mariah's suspicions. She took cultures, wrote orders for admission, and started high-potency, broad-spectrum intravenous antibiotics.

Mariah thought of another option for Rose in addition to radiation. If the cancer had not spread to her pelvic bones, she could undergo an operation called "pelvic exenteration." This surgery was designed to cure patients whose cervical cancer invaded the tissues near the cervix and uterus but had not spread to the bones or the rest of the body. A pelvic exenteration removed the bladder, colon, and rectum, leaving the patient with two bags and a huge scar—but alive and potentially cancer-free. This complex, multispecialty surgery was performed only at select medical centers across the country. Mariah decided to discuss this case with Dave Mettson first.

Once the paperwork and dictation were completed, Mariah went back to labor and delivery. It was 6:45 p.m., and the dining hall closed at 6:30. She had missed dinner!

Maybel Thompson approached Maria on labor and delivery to give her an update, and Mariah interrupted, "Is there any food available for doctors to eat if they miss dinner at the dining hall?"

Maybel smiled, picked up the telephone receiver, and started dialing the kitchen. "I'll order you a dinner tray." Maybel was the most experienced civilian labor and delivery nurse at MACH. She was in her sixties, tall with white hair that framed a beautiful face, high cheekbones, and penetrating dark-brown eyes. Her most valuable trait, however, was an assertive yet friendly character that cut through the mayhem and took control in stressful situations. "You can get a turkey platter with gravy, mashed potatoes, and green beans. We always order a few extra trays for the patients who deliver in the evening so they have a meal. But we need to order soon, before the kitchen crew leaves."

Mariah added. "Can I get a dinner tray *without* meat?"

Maybel's eyes ran up and down Mariah's thin frame with barely concealed disapproval as she put the phone to her ear. "You don't eat meat? Are you one of those vegetarians?" Her southern drawl lengthened with indignation. "Well, maybe we can get you a cheese sandwich or something. You can eat cheese, right?"

"Yes, thanks. *Two* cheese sandwiches would be great."

"I'll see what I can do." Maybel shook her head and then remembered what she was going to tell Mariah.

"Oh, and room one is about to deliver."

Twenty minutes later, Mariah delivered a baby boy. He was big and healthy, and his father cried as he held him in his arms.

The second patient was more complicated. Mariah had begun Pitocin to strengthen her contractions prior to seeing Rose. After being on the Pitocin for several hours, the patient's contractions were strong again. She had an epidural to keep her comfortable while her contractions continued, but her cervix still hadn't dilated. Mariah began discussing C-section as the next step for delivery.

At first her patient was worried about having a C-section. She listened as Mariah explained the procedure and risks, and began to feel comfortable with the plan. She signed the consent form, and Mariah left to call the OR.

Where's my sandwich? Mariah wondered. It was 8:00 p.m., and she could really use something to eat before she started this case. She walked through the nurses' station and asked, "Has anyone seen my dinner tray? It had two cheese sandwiches."

"Oh! Was that yours? I gave it to the patient who just delivered." The nurse picked up the phone. "I'm sorry. Let me get you another one before the kitchen crew goes home for the night. What time is it? Is it after seven thirty? Because they go home at seven thirty, and there won't be anyone to make you a sandwich."

"It's 8:00 p.m." Mariah sighed and opened a small refrigerator that held snacks for laboring patients. All she could find was vanilla pudding. She took two cups and started down the back stairs to the OR.

Smaller hospitals, like MACH, didn't have a dedicated operating room for C-sections. When a labor patient needed a C-section, she was wheeled in her labor bed to the operating room, often on a completely different floor. In emergencies, if there wasn't time to move the patient, a C-section might be performed in the delivery room using an old anesthesia monitor or just local anesthetic.

The C-section went smoothly. After completing the paperwork, Mariah returned to labor and delivery to ensure all was quiet before lying down in her call room. She was exhausted and fell into a wonderful black hole of sleep.

The alarm jolted her awake at 6:00 a.m. Sun was streaming in through the small window near the ceiling in the call room like it was a prison cell. She pulled herself out of bed and rummaged through her call bag, looking for her toiletries. No matter how tired, hungry, or behind schedule she was, she always made time for a shower. The hot water washed away her fatigue and the day always seemed brighter once she was toweled off and dressed in clean clothes.

MACH required providers who were on call the night before to work half a day in clinic. By two o'clock, Mariah was singing to the radio, driving Irving home.

She opened the door to their apartment and called, "Hello!" as she entered.

Emery was sitting on the floor, busy trying to assemble an IKEA bookshelf for their apartment. He wanted to get all the boxes unpacked before he began his new job in Atlanta. Looking up from the clutter of boards and screws, he smiled. "'Some assembly required' is a joke. I should have bought a few boards, a saw, and some nails. How was your first and second day of work?" He rose from his pile of debris and gave Mariah a hug and a kiss.

"It was a typical night on call. 'Mitchell' is a pretty busy hospital." Mariah changed out of her work clothes. "I'm tired and hungry. Do you mind if we have an early dinner?"

"Not at all. In fact, let's go out. There's a Japanese steak house that I want to try, and I think you can get sushi there."

Mariah wasn't eager for sushi from a steak house in the middle of Georgia. "Or maybe fried rice."

As they drove to the restaurant, Mariah couldn't help smiling. It was nice to live together and enjoy life as a couple. The unpacking was a lot of work, but their apartment was becoming cozy. She was happy everything was coming together so well. She crossed her legs, sat back in her seat, and sang along with the radio.

Chapter Twelve

Rose Bouton responded to the IV antibiotics and was discharged home after two days in the hospital. She returned with her husband to see Mariah at the end of the week.

Hank was a tall man with dark hair pulled back in a thin ponytail. Mariah wondered about Hank's prior service. Was he wounded in a prior conflict and retired? Regardless, his drawn manner was in direct conflict with Rose's enthusiasm. She looked hopeful as she held her husband's hand and waited for Mariah to speak. Hank, on the other hand, looked lost sitting next to Rose in the small exam room.

Before Mariah could begin, Hank asked, "Dr. Gordon, can I ask a question, please?"

"Of course, Mr. Bouton." Mariah pulled up her stool and sat down. "What's your question?"

"When Rose had her surgery at the county hospital, they referred to her cervical cancer as HPV. I'm not familiar with HPV, but I heard it called an STD. My questions is this: Why is my wife, who is having surgery for cervical cancer, being diagnosed with an STD?"

Mariah took a deep breath and began, "That's a good question. Human papilloma virus, or HPV, is a very common virus. Almost everyone who has ever had sex has been infected with it, but they don't know it because they usually have no symptoms, and the vast majority of infections resolve spontaneously. HPV is a wart virus and is passed by skin-to-skin contact, including sex. Condoms don't completely protect against HPV. There are over one hundred subtypes of HPV; some subtypes cause genital warts, some cause cervical cancer, and others can cause other cancers, like penile or oral cancer."

Mariah continued, "Cervical cancer develops from the HPV virus. Only a small percentage of women infected with HPV develop cervical cancer. The body clears ninety percent of all HPV infections before anyone knows they're infected. Of the ten percent of HPV infections that are not cleared, about half become dormant, and half become precancerous. This process takes years, and regular Pap smear screening will detect precancerous changes long before they become cancer."

Rose interrupted. "I didn't get a Pap smear for ten years after I delivered Emily," she confided, looking at the floor. "A few months ago, I started bleeding and came here for an appointment. That's when they found I had cervical cancer."

Mariah comforted Rose. "What's done is done. You can call it an STD, but if having sex is human, then being exposed to HPV is human, too." Mariah needed to change the subject and focus on treating Rose.

Mariah had contacted Dr. David Mettson, the gynecologic oncology expert from her residency who was now stationed at Walter Reed. She picked up Rose's chart and began to explain why Rose should consider another surgery. "If Rose's cancer has not spread into her pelvic bones or beyond, she would be a great candidate for a 'pelvic exenteration' surgery. All the organs in her pelvis would be removed, and she would have a bag for her bladder and a bag for her bowel movements, but her survival could be much longer."

Mariah knew Rose had few options and wanted her to know all the choices available. "If you both agree, we will refer Rose to Walter Reed Medical Center for an evaluation to determine if she is eligible for this surgery. Dr. Mettson's office will arrange the appointments. All you have to arrange is your travel." Mariah looked at them both.

Hank looked up from studying the floor tiles. "You really think this surgery could work? It could remove all the cancer and stop her pain?"

Much to Mariah's surprise, Hank broke out into a cautious smile. This tall, stern hulk of a man gently took his wife's hand and looked into her eyes. His expression was suddenly full of hope and love. It was obvious that Rose was his life and he would do whatever it took to keep her alive.

He turned to Mariah. "We'll go to Walter Reed. Just tell me when and where, and I'll get her there."

Mariah exhaled. She had not imagined Rose's family declining this challenging proposal, but when she first saw this man's manner, she became unsure.

Rose's appointment took a long time, and Mariah's next patient, Specialist Barbara Cohen, had been waiting for over half an hour. The consult form on her chart read, "Abnormal Pap Smear."

Another HPV explanation, Mariah thought, knowing these conversations often took longer than the allotted appointment time. *I'll never catch up.*

Barbara was twenty-three years old, and her Pap read: "Low-grade squamous intraepithelial lesion with changes consistent with HPV." She was scared and upset and wanted to know what this meant. Mariah knew that, like Hank, she was wondering if having HPV meant that she had cervical cancer or an STD.

Before Mariah could begin, Barbara started to cry. "I don't understand how I got HPV. I've always been so careful. Did my boyfriend give it to me, because he says he doesn't have it, and I must have gotten it from someone else." Barbara sniffed and grabbed a tissue.

Mariah handed her the whole box of Kleenex. "Don't cry, Barbara. Let me explain, and you'll see that things are really not that bad. Let's talk about HPV first, and then we'll talk about your Pap smear result."

Mariah repeated her HPV explanation concluding with the statement, "That means you, your boyfriend, your old boyfriends, and his old girlfriends; almost everyone has been infected with HPV."

"How come I never heard about it?" Barbara asked. "Why isn't this information on the news or something?"

"I don't know, but I think it's because it has to do with sex and people can't get past that fact."

Barbara sniffed again. "Isn't HPV an STD?"

"HPV is transmitted sexually, but having it doesn't mean someone is dirty or promiscuous. In our culture and as human beings, sex is common and considered normal between consenting adults, and the prevalence of HPV exposure should not be surprising."

Mariah needed to move on. "Ninety percent of everyone infected with HPV overcome their infection. 'Low-grade' or mildly abnormal changes like those on your Pap smear are common in young women and often go away on their own. Your body's immune system will usually clear up these infections in six months to a year."

"All you need to do," Mariah continued, "is follow a healthy lifestyle to support your immune system. Healthy diet, exercise, and no smoking. Not even sidestream smoke." Mariah could see she struck a chord. "You don't smoke, do you?"

Barbara pulled her pack of cigarettes out of her purse. "Yes, but I don't smoke that much." She slipped the cigarettes into the trashcan next to the desk. "I'm going to quit today."

"Good, because smoking makes the HPV much stronger and harder for your body to fight. So today we don't need to do anything but schedule a repeat Pap smear in one year." Mariah stood up, signaling the conclusion of the consult.

"I have to wait a year?" Barbara stayed seated and looked unhappy. "How will I know it's not growing inside me? I can't wait that long. Can't you just remove the abnormal cells now?"

Mariah sat back down. "Barbara, two-thirds of all Pap smears like yours will resolve on their own. And if it doesn't resolve, it is very unlikely to progress. If we remove those cells, we could harm your cervix unnecessarily. The research is sound and you must trust me; it is better for you to wait and repeat the Pap smear in a year. If you want to do something helpful, quit smoking."

"What about my boyfriend—should we use condoms?"

"Condoms don't completely protect against the transmission of HPV. Remember what I told you; almost everyone who has ever had sex has been infected with HPV. He probably has HPV, too. Quit smoking, be healthy, and repeat your Pap smear in a year."

Barbara looked a little skeptical as Mariah escorted her to the scheduling desk to make her appointment.

"Here, give this pamphlet to your boyfriend, too." Mariah handed her two pamphlets on HPV.

Chapter Thirteen

It was 6:30 a.m. Friday, and the scent of freshly brewed coffee filled the kitchen. Mariah savored a few quiet moments sipping coffee at the kitchen table with Emery. He was not a morning person, and she knew he went back to bed after she left, but she appreciated seeing his tired smile and crazy bedhead before going to work. Living together was fun. Their first week flew by without a single argument as they unpacked and settled into their apartment.

Emery's new job with a law firm in Atlanta started next week. He planned to use the free time to unpack all their boxes, assemble shelves, and put everything away. He also found the closest airfield with a flight school and arranged some flying time. Mariah was on call this weekend, and he planned to fly while she worked.

"Have fun today." Mariah smiled as she finished her coffee and put her mug in the sink. "I'll be home tomorrow morning. I'm not sure what time Dr. Parsons will relieve me."

"Emptying boxes and putting up shelves is not my idea of fun, but I should have everything put away before you get home. Oh, and I'll probably get home after you tomorrow; I have my first flight with the flying school at 8:00 a.m." Emery followed her to the coffeemaker and poured himself another cup of coffee.

"Isn't that a little early for you?" She smiled.

"It is. But they told me it's better to fly early during the summer, before it gets too hot. Do you want a travel mug?" He held up the coffeepot.

"Yes, please. I'll probably take a nap when I get home, anyway. What do you want to do in the afternoon?" Mariah picked up her call bag and briefcase.

"Let's see how tired you are. We could go to a movie or just rent a video. Let's play it by ear." He handed her the travel mug and followed her to the front door. "Have a good day. Love you." And he kissed her good-bye.

"I love you, too. And be careful tomorrow." Mariah turned and walked to her car, smiling.

When Mariah arrived at the hospital, there were two labor patients on labor and delivery. She was on call for the weekend and took over the care and management of all the OB-GYN patients admitted to the hospital. Dr. Jane Kennedy was on call the night before and signed out all the patients to Mariah. In addition to the two women in labor, there were five postpartum patients and two postoperative GYN patients. Mariah made rounds and discharged everyone except for two postpartum patients who had delivered yesterday. The two patients in labor progressed at different rates, and by 4:00 p.m., one had delivered and the other was on Pitocin.

Mariah sat at labor and delivery's workstation, watching the fetal monitors and the clock. It had been a calm, slow day, and she didn't want to miss dinner. It felt cool on labor and delivery, and Mariah was just about to put on her pink fuzzy sweater when a group of men in uniform came down the hall toward labor and delivery's nursing station.

"Here comes the commander," Maybel whispered as she got up and smoothed her scrub jacket.

"Why is he *here*?" Mariah whispered. In residency, the hospital commander often visited the burn unit or the med-surg wards, but he never visited labor and delivery.

"Colonel Riley walks through the hospital all the time. He likes to visit and see everyone working. I think he's a good commander..." Maybel cut her compliment short and greeted the officers. "Good afternoon, Commander."

"Good afternoon, Nurse Thompson." Colonel Norman Riley smiled and shook Maybel's hand. "How is everything on labor and delivery today? I see our new ob-gyn doctor is hard at work!"

He smiled and extended his hand to Mariah. "It's nice to meet you, Dr. Gordon. I'm Colonel Riley."

"It's nice to meet you, too." Mariah shook his hand and smiled. The commander was younger and more handsome than she expected.

Unintentionally, Mariah showed a lack of respect for the commander by omitting the customary "sir" phrase used with superior officers. She noticed the two field officers standing with the colonel were not impressed. Mariah's four years of active duty army service were spent entirely in the hospital, and with the exception of airborne training and ROTC, she almost never spoke to regular army officers. Realizing her blunder too late for a correction, she concentrated on remembering to add "sir" the next time she spoke.

"I hope you're finding everything OK. If you have a question that you think I can answer, don't hesitate to call me." Colonel Riley started to turn to go.

Mariah realized she was going to lose her opportunity and blurted out, "Thank you, sir!"

Smiling, Colonel Riley added, "If something unexpected happens on labor and delivery, I want to be informed. Even if that means calling me at home in the middle of the night, understand?" He looked her straight in the eye.

"Yes, sir. It was nice meeting you, sir."

Mariah waited another ten minutes after the officers left labor and delivery before going down to the dining hall. She wanted to be sure she would not run into any of them again. As she entered the dining hall, she swore under her breath. There was Colonel Riley! Why was he eating in the hospital cafeteria on a Friday night? He ordered meatloaf, mashed potatoes, and green beans, and then gave her a quick smile. Mariah smiled back.

The specialist behind the counter asked, "What would you like Ma'am? Turkey or meatloaf?"

Mariah spoke softly, "Just mashed potatoes and green beans, please."

"Are you on call tonight?" Colonel Riley was holding his tray full of food and trying to make conversation as she grabbed a slice of chocolate cake.

"Yes," she said as she pulled a few dollars out of her pocket. Realizing she had forgotten the "sir" again, she added, "I hope it's a quiet night. Have a good night, sir."

Mariah picked up her tray and walked out of the dining hall toward labor and delivery. In the hospital, everyone was laid back about rank. Doctors were called "doctor," not "captain," "major," or "colonel." But in the regular army, rank really mattered, and it was important to show respect.

At the nurses' station, Mariah ate while watching the fetal monitor. She took a bite of her chocolate cake and felt eyes looking at her.

A young blond woman, wearing a long white lab coat with a stethoscope around her neck, extended her hand to Mariah. "Hi, Dr. Gordon. I'm Sheila Roberts, the family practice resident on call for labor and delivery tonight."

"Nice to meet you, Sheila. Please call me Mariah. What year are you in residency?" Mariah shook the pretty young doctor's hand and wondered why there had been no resident on call with her Monday night when she could have used the help.

"Third year. I'm a chief, so I'd like to do all the vaginal deliveries myself—if that's OK with you." Her dark-brown eyes were intent, and Mariah was glad to have a motivated resident on call with her.

"That's fine with me. How many deliveries have you done?"

"Fifty-five. And I've assisted on four C-sections," Sheila spoke proudly.

Family practice residencies lasted three years, and Sheila was just beginning her final, chief year.

"Well, this patient could go either way." Mariah pointed to the fetal heart rate tracing on the monitor. "She has been four centimeters for three hours, and I just started Pitocin after evaluating her. What are the things I was looking for in my evaluation?" Mariah quizzed her, trying to determine her knowledge of obstetrics besides delivering babies.

"You would evaluate her baby for distress, her pelvis for adequate birth canal, and the strength of her contractions," Sheila responded quickly and smiled. "OB is my favorite rotation."

"Excellent! We'll have a lot of fun together." Mariah smiled, too.

The phone rang, and the labor and delivery clerk interrupted them. "That was the ER calling to give us a heads up; they're sending up a woman in labor. She's six centimeters dilated, and it's her fifth baby. Her name is Sylvia Martin, and she's followed in the family practice clinic. I'll pull her OB chart."

Maybel got up and inspected the closest vacant labor room. The bedsheets were turned down, and the fetal and uterine contraction monitors lay on top, ready to be strapped onto the next patient. "Let's put her in room two." She turned on the lights, powered up the monitors, and opened an IV kit.

The ER orderly appeared a moment later, pushing a very uncomfortable-looking woman in a wheelchair down the hall toward their nurses' station.

"Straight to room two," Maybel called and pointed the orderly toward her room.

Mariah stared at the woman's belly as she went by; it looked *too* big. The orderly placed her ER paperwork on the counter as he wheeled his groaning patient past the nurses' station.

The labor and delivery clerk placed a thin OB chart on top of the ER paperwork and declared, "That's all we've got on her."

OB patients are seen routinely in offices and clinics, yet ultimately are delivered on labor and delivery. Every night, all the charts must be available to the labor and delivery staff in case of an emergency or labor. At MACH, the OB charts were stored in mobile cabinets on labor and delivery at night and rolled to clinic in the morning.

Sylvia Martin's entire OB chart consisted of two pages. The first page listed blood test results, and the second page documented her initial OB appointment, six months ago.

Sylvia was defiant while Maybel placed an IV in her arm. "I have four kids at home and no money for a babysitter. How am I supposed to go to OB appointments with all those kids?" She began panting between contractions. "Besides, all my pregnancies went fine. Those doctors never did nothin' but listen to the baby and check my blood pressure. I don't need no damn OB appointment for that."

Mariah studied Sylvia's large abdomen and then glanced at her scanty chart. "Your labs *were* normal except for some mild anemia. According to the chart, you are due in four weeks, but your belly looks very large to me. Do you mind if I do a quick ultrasound?"

"Is there something wrong with my baby?" Sylvia's defiance dissolved into concern for her unborn baby.

"No, ma'am," Mariah soothed her. "I just want to look at your baby with the ultrasound. And we need to check your cervix again."

"OK. And I want some pain medicine!" Sylvia called as Mariah went to get the portable ultrasound machine. "Not that epidermal thing in my back, just morphine!" She started breathing again through her next contraction.

Mariah turned on the ultrasound machine, and while it warmed up, Sheila checked Sylvia's cervix.

"You're eight centimeters dilated," Sheila announced as Mariah squirted ultrasound gel on Sylvia's swollen belly.

The ultrasound machine was old, and the picture was grainy. Mariah explained what she saw on the screen to Sylvia. "This baby is in good position to deliver first, and we'll call her Baby A for now. And the other baby,

Baby B, is over here. Definitely a boy! He's also in good position to follow his sister."

Mariah winked at Maybel and Sheila as she pointed with the transducer. "Maybel, can you please put a fetal monitor on Baby B? His heart is right here."

"What did you say?" Sylvia was up on her elbows, trying to see the ultrasound screen over her belly. "Are you saying I have twins? I can't deliver two babies! I want a C-section! Just knock me out and take them. And tie my tubes while you're at it!" She leaned back and started to cry.

Mariah patted Sylvia's hand and watched Baby B's heart rate begin to appear on the monitor. "Don't cry. You're going to be OK. Did someone come with you to the hospital?"

Delivering twins was high risk. Mariah needed to call in a pediatrician as well as the OR crew and anesthesia doctor in case of an emergency during delivery. Sylvia stopped crying and groaned with her next contraction— they didn't have much time.

"No. Drove myself. Husband stayed home with the kids." She was breathing again and starting to push.

"We have to move her to the delivery room. Now!" Mariah unlocked the bed and called to the labor and delivery clerk as they wheeled Sylvia past her to the delivery room, "Page the pediatrician and anesthesiologist on call. Let them know we have thirty-six-week twins delivering now. Tell the OR to be on standby in case we need them, and call the OB clinic. Tell them to have Dr.

Samuelson or Morales stand by in the hospital until the babies are delivered. Let them know I have another patient on Pitocin, too."

Sheila had everything ready in the delivery room and held the doors open as they wheeled in Sylvia on her labor bed. Two infant resuscitation units were warming, a delivery table was set up, and a C-section surgery pack was pulled out, just in case. Mariah pulled the ultrasound into the delivery room and began to scrub her hands. Sheila helped move the patient onto a delivery table and then joined Mariah at the scrub sink.

Mariah smiled to diffuse the tension and asked, "Have you done any twin deliveries, yet?"

"I've delivered two Baby A's, but both times the mother needed a C-section to deliver the second twin." Sheila sounded disappointed.

"Let's hope we don't need to do a C-section this time." Mariah held her wet arms up and backed into the delivery room. She dried her arms, and gowned and gloved herself as the OR crew arrived.

Surveying the activity in the delivery room, Mariah was happy to see how quickly everything was made ready for the twin delivery. Dr. Gottlieb, the pediatrician, was testing the newborn resuscitation equipment, and Dr. Lamont, the anesthesiologist, was talking to Sylvia, calmly taking her history and talking about her options for pain control. The babies' heart rate tracings looked reassuring, and Mariah turned to discuss her delivery plan with Sheila.

"You deliver twin A, and I'll stand by with the ultrasound on Twin B. Don't collect cord blood; instead, clamp the cord with this plastic clamp and wait for me. I'll monitor Baby B's heartbeat and guide his head down into her pelvis. When I tell you, I want you to break the second sac and place a scalp electrode on Baby B. Any questions?"

"No."

Sylvia had another contraction, and this time she couldn't help but push with all her strength. Baby A was much smaller than her prior babies and delivered easily. Mariah placed the ultrasound transducer on Sylvia's partially deflated tummy, checked Baby B's heart rate, and guided his head down toward Sylvia's pelvis.

"The heartbeat looks good," Mariah called out to everyone in the room. "Here comes another contraction."

Sylvia pushed Baby B down into her birth canal, and two contractions later, Baby B delivered. Sheila was thrilled, Mariah was relieved, and Sylvia was crying, this time for joy. Both babies were small but healthy, and Dr. Gottlieb planned close surveillance primarily due to their lack of prenatal care.

Mariah let Sheila do all the delivery paperwork and went to check on the other labor patient. She was six centimeters and wanted an epidural.

"Dr. Lamont!" Mariah called as he was leaving labor and delivery. "My patient in room three wants an epidural."

He turned around and smiled as he walked back toward the nurses' station. "I should have checked. Thanks for catching me before I got in my car. Any chance she's going to need a C-section later?" Anesthesia doctors always asked that question.

"I left my crystal ball at home, but I don't think I'll need to call you back for a C-section later. At least not for her." Mariah smiled.

By ten o'clock, all the patients were delivered, everything was quiet, and Mariah went to bed. Sheila sat in the nurses' station reading about twin deliveries.

At 5:00 a.m. Mariah awoke, anxious to go home. She ate breakfast, rounded on all her patients, and sat reading the newspaper on labor and delivery until Dr. Parsons arrived. She heard he had a busy private OB-GYN practice in Columbus and wondered why he would want to take extra call on Saturday.

At eleven o'clock, he walked up to the nurses' station wearing expensive clothes and a winning white smile. "Hello, everybody! You must be Dr. Gordon." He extended his hand to Mariah.

"Nice to meet you, Dr. Parsons. Please call me Mariah."

"You can call me Brad. What do you have going on for me today?" He rubbed his hands together and looked around in anticipation.

"Not much. We delivered twins and a singleton last night, and everyone on the floor is doing well. It's been quiet this morning." Mariah picked up her call bag and briefcase, anxious to leave. "See you tomorrow."

Even though she had slept most of the night at the hospital, Mariah was still tired. As planned, she took a nap while Emery went flying. He picked up a video on the way home. Mariah was nervous about being tired on Sunday, so they enjoyed an easy afternoon on the couch together and went to bed early.

Chapter Fourteen

Sunday morning was quiet at MACH, with no one in labor. Mariah took advantage of the downtime to finish unpacking her office, and invited Emery to have lunch with her at the hospital. While unpacking a box of textbooks, she discovered journal articles about team-safety practices in aviation. Emery had handed these to her as she was packing back in Texas; he felt health care could benefit from teamwork training. The articles addressed teamwork training used by the aviation industry. Reading the articles reminded Mariah about the communication errors that complicated the care for Penny and Captain Stevens. She decided to bring the subject up at lunch.

Emery sat in the dining hall, looking at the food on his tray. "How can you eat this stuff? Oh, I forgot, you probably don't eat much of it, do you?"

Mariah sighed and pushed her salad around her plate. "It's hard to be a vegetarian in the army. But I don't support factory farming." She ate a forkful of lettuce. "I found the articles you gave me on teamwork training. They were very interesting, especially after Captain Stevens's ultrasound report was lost for three days."

Emery smiled as he chewed his sandwich. He had read more on the topic. "Have you heard of the 'Swiss Cheese Model'?"

Mariah replied, "Not yet."

Emery went on eagerly. "The Swiss Cheese Model explains how people can be harmed even when there are several good safety practices in place. Every safety practice has several domains that make it work: for example, supervision, organization, specific acts, and preconditions. Each domain has 'holes' in its integrity, or times when it can be compromised: a supervisor is called away, communication breaks down, staffing shortage, human error.

"If several holes in the safety practice domains line up, an accident can occur, like Flight 173 running out of fuel and crashing while trying to problem-solve a landing gear issue. Fuel gauge lights and alarms are designed to prevent the disastrous consequence of a plane running out of fuel while flying. But failure in the cockpit's organization and communication caused the warning signals to be ignored and allowed the catastrophe to occur.

"Maybe the same thing happened with your patient, Penny. When a catastrophe like that occurs, it's called a 'sentinel event' or 'never event' because it never should have happened."

Mariah reflected, "I can see how several factors lined up in Penny's case: poor communication, lack of supervision, and lack of monitoring. Although safety practices were in place, they failed to identify when her baby was in distress; nothing was known until it was too late."

Emery continued, "Sentinel events are catastrophic events that often involve multiple failures of safety nets to pick up a problem. The goal is to identify the root causes of 'sentinel events' to determine common failures. Once these common areas of failure are identified and studied, changes can be made to prevent future failures."

"What are the most common areas of failure in aviation?" Mariah was almost afraid to encourage him.

"Lack of communication and teamwork. Most sentinel events involve a breakdown of communication and hierarchy in the cockpit that inhibits teamwork. Improving communication and empowering all team members to play an active role decreased the incidence of sentinel events. The FAA implemented communication and team-based training, and decreased the number of plane crashes."

Emery took another bite of his sandwich. "Medicine would benefit tremendously from this approach, but it means that doctors, like pilots, need to replace the idea of being 'captain of the ship' with being 'leader' of the ship."

Mariah chuckled as she imagined Dr. Halligan communicating with each resident on his team instead of just barking orders to the chief resident and disappearing into his office. Applying a team approach to patient safety was compelling.

Emery concluded, "As the responsible and most knowledgeable member of the health care team, the doctor must assume the leadership role. They must lead all the members of their team to provide the best care possible for each patient.

He stood up and kissed her on the forehead. "I have to go. Tomorrow's my first day at work, and I need to get ready."

Mariah followed him out of the dining hall to MACH's front entrance. After a quick hug, she turned and walked toward her office inside the empty GYN clinic. She always felt most lonely right after Emery left. To occupy herself, she decided to develop a teamwork plan for patient care at MACH.

Emery's articles described CRM as the strategy used to create a "safety-first" work environment by encouraging situational awareness, assertiveness, and communication from every member of the team. Mariah employed some of CRM's tools and developed a simple safety program for both labor and delivery and the OR. Incorporating the CRM strategy into the practice of hospital health care seemed like an idea whose time had come.

Mariah imagined the largest obstacle to changing the structure of patient care from hierarchy to a team-based system was the medical staff. Research showed that hierarchy prevented good communication practices among team members, yet its use was entrenched in the practice of medicine. In light of the increasing complexities of modern medicine, it was irrational to assume one person could know everything and be infallible. Root-cause analysis showed over and over again that performing complex functions in areas of high criticality was best done with a team approach. Despite the facts and evidence, Mariah knew it would be difficult to convince the doctors to change their approach from "captain of the ship" to "leader of a team."

Later Sunday afternoon, while sipping coffee at the nurses' station on labor and delivery, Mariah tested the nurses' attitudes about teamwork in patient care by outlining her patient safety plan. Empowering nurses to speak up to ensure safe practices were being employed was unconventional. Mariah wondered if this might be difficult for them.

Maybel was the first to speak up. "That makes so much sense. I would love to see the look on Dr. Samuelson's face when I tell him calmly, 'I think it's time for a C-section.' Instead, I have to wait until he finally understands what I already knew and yells, 'Stat C-section!' We're all behind you on this one, one hundred percent, Dr. Gordon."

The ER called while Mariah sat chatting with the nurses, A woman in labor was on her way up, and they had a GYN patient for Mariah to see in room three.

"Time to get back to work!" Mariah tossed her coffee cup in the trash and put on her white lab coat.

Sunday night was busy, and Monday morning's clinic was full. Mariah drove home tired but excited about her patient safety idea. She stopped at a grocery store and bought tuna steaks and a key lime pie, planning to cook a nice dinner to celebrate Emery's first day of work.

"Wake up, Mariah." Emery shook her gently.

Mariah blinked as he turned on the bedroom light, and noticed it was dark outside. "When did you get home?"

"Half an hour ago. I cooked the tuna steaks and can't wait to eat any longer. Get up!"

"OK, OK." Mariah rose and the full weight of her fatigue hit her like a punch in the temple. Her head pounded and her joints ached for more rest. "I feel awful. Hope I'm not getting sick, no time for that."

Mariah shuffled to the table. The fish was smothered in a mango salsa with baby red potatoes sautéed in butter and dill. It smelled delightful, and Mariah remembered she had skipped lunch; maybe she felt rotten because she was hungry. She began eating, oblivious to Emery sitting across from her, his wine glass poised in the air, waiting for a mutual toast and a "clink" to start the meal.

His silent gaze produced an awkwardness that even Mariah's obtuse social skills perceived. She glanced up at him while bringing her fork to her lips.

"Oops! Sorry. Here's to you for making such a wonderful meal. Thanks, Emery, you really outdid yourself."

"Here's to us. You made it through your first week of work, and I survived my first day at the law firm."

Emery smiled and raised his wine glass high. Mariah clinked and slowed her eating to savor the flavors and enjoy the conversation about Emery's new office.

That night, Rose Bouton's daughter appeared in a nightmare that awoke Mariah from sleep. Emily was crying and running frantically through the crowded ER, calling for her mother. Once awake, the image of Emily's tear-streaked face haunted Mariah. Afraid the dream might recur if she went back to sleep, Mariah quietly got up and went to the kitchen.

Moonlight streamed in through the windows of the new apartment, and everything looked foreign. Sitting alone in the dark, Mariah reflected on the vividness of her dream. She hadn't heard from David Mettson yet, but she felt sure that Rose must already be at Walter Reed Medical Center undergoing her evaluation. Mariah shuddered at the images of Rose's panicking daughter and hoped Rose could be cured with surgery.

Quietly, she opened the refrigerator, took out the key lime pie, and cut a big slice for herself. Eating always made her feel better after a nightmare.

Snap! The kitchen lights came on as Emery flipped the switch and illuminated Mariah's midnight snack.

"Are you eating my pie?" Emery feigned anger, snatching her empty plate and going to the refrigerator. "Want another piece?" He smiled over his shoulder.

"OK. Key lime pie never tastes as good the second day, anyway." Mariah smiled. It was nice to have the diversion from her nightmare. She leaned over and kissed him on the nose with sticky, key lime–smeared lips.

"Thanks." he said and wiped off his face.

Chapter Fifteen

The Georgia heat melted July into August, and Mariah was happy to work indoors all day. By the end of the day her car was like a furnace, blasting heat into her face as she opened the car door. Irving's black vinyl seats and steering wheel threatened to sear her skin. Trying to reflect some of the heat, Mariah used dishtowels to cover the seat and steering wheel while Irving broiled all day in the parking lot.

Hoping for relief from the heat, Mariah and Emery put on bathing suits and investigated their apartment's outdoor pool. It was crowded with mothers holding babies in diapers, and small children splashing each other. Mariah wondered how diapers could be effective in a pool. Turning back without ever touching the water, they decided to avoid the pool altogether and went to a movie instead. Popcorn and air-conditioning made even the most boring movie seem like a nice experience.

Summer passed quickly, and Mariah was happy. Her patients loved her and wrote complimentary reviews about her to the commander. Dr. Morales enjoyed reminding Mariah how good she made him look as he passed the commander's comment cards back to Mariah. The nurses on labor and delivery were always happy when she was on call, and Mariah made some friends in the OR.

Dr. Morales put Mariah in charge of teaching OB-GYN to the family practice residents. Her fast smile and fun teaching style made her their favorite teacher.

Autumn brought cooler days and the end of Mariah's honeymoon at MACH. Instead of seeing patients in the ER while on call, Dr. Morales began scheduling them to see Mariah in clinic, sometimes the same day. Mariah's clinic schedules became overbooked with complicated patients, often acutely sick, needing surgery the same day they were seen.

Dr. Ken Samuelson was unwilling to help. Mariah had hoped Ken would be a mentor, but he was burned out and couldn't wait to leave. He looked forward to completing his army commitment and often took leave to interview for jobs. The staff in the clinic told Mariah he planned to join a private practice in Virginia next July.

Dr. Jane Kennedy was burned out too. She balked if any patient issues were not solved by the time she took over night call. Mariah was pressured to deliver her patients, complete any evaluations, and run down any details before she signed out each evening. In October, Mariah discovered Dr. Kennedy was also rescheduling her difficult patients with Mariah.

Holding a copy of her schedule, Mariah walked into Dr. Kennedy's office demanding, "Why is your GYN patient scheduled to see me? Mrs. Ravens had surgery with you three months ago for pelvic pain. Now she has an appointment for chronic pelvic pain in my GYN clinic."

Dr. Kennedy faced Mariah with an innocent expression. "Since you're new and still building your practice, I thought you might benefit from an extra patient. If you don't want to see her, I'll have them change her appointment."

Is she implying that I'm lazy? "My clinic is always full. I don't need extra patients to keep me busy."

After a long day of work, Mariah often came home tired and moody.

"Why do I always have to pick up after you?" Mariah complained as she walked around the apartment on a Saturday morning collecting coffee mugs and beer bottles. "I feel like I spend what little free time I have cleaning up after you." She stood looking in the messy kitchen. "I love it when you cook, but do you have to use every pot?"

Emery looked up from a law brief he was reading. As the junior member of his law firm, he too was struggling with an excessive workload and frequently brought work home on the weekends. And the two-hour commute to Atlanta took its toll on his patience.

He frowned. "Don't pick up after me, just leave it. I'll pick it up later. You're welcome for all the dinners I cooked. You cook dinner from now on—I get home too late anyway." He looked at his watch and started packing up his briefcase. "Time to go. I scheduled a few hours of flying time."

"You're going flying now?" Mariah was surprised and hurt that he was going flying instead of spending time with her. "I thought we had the whole day together. I can't believe you'd rather spend time up in that plane than with me."

Emery became defensive. "I thought you were going to clean." Then he quickly added, "I don't have much free time either, and I love to fly. Can't you amuse yourself for the afternoon? Let's catch a movie later."

Furious, Mariah spat, "I don't want to go to a movie. I wanted to spend time with you."

Emery shot back, "You want me to cancel my flying time?"

Mariah refused to admit it and said instead, "No. I guess I made a mistake."

Now Emery was mad. "What's that supposed to mean?"

"Just go." Mariah put the coffee mugs and beer bottles in the sink walked into the bedroom, and slammed the door shut. She waited, hoping to hear his footstep near the door or the doorknob turn. Instead, the front door slammed. Angry and hurt, Mariah started to cry.

They made up that night, but she still felt wounded, and the fighting continued. Mariah felt their relationship was stressed but not in trouble—until she came home late one night and found Emery sitting alone at the kitchen table, in the dark.

"Why are you sitting in the dark?" she asked.

"It wasn't dark when you called and said you were leaving the hospital and would be home in twenty minutes—that was two hours ago."

Mariah became defensive. "I got paged. My surgical patient spiked a fever, and I couldn't leave without evaluating her. Jane is on call tonight, and she's such a jerk if I sign out any work for her." Mariah conceded, "I'm sorry I'm late."

Emery wasn't finished. "I feel like I always come last—after your job *and* your colleagues."

Mariah could see that he was hurt. She wanted to tell him how much she loved him and thought of him all day at work. But she chose to be a doctor, and sacrifices of personal time had to be made. Emery needed to understand this, too.

Instead of empathizing with how Emery felt, Mariah became frustrated. *Why was Emery aggravating her before she was even in the door?* She thought to herself, *Emery should know how I feel about him; I asked him to move in with me, didn't I?* "That's ridiculous. I love you very much, and I always put you first, or at least ahead of me. I just can't put you or me ahead of a patient's care."

Mariah didn't say another word. Instead, she walked past him and started dinner.

Stress was eating away at their relationship. Mariah knew she was hard to live with but couldn't tame her temper. She blamed her outbursts on her job and hoped everything would improve once Dr. Kennedy left in March. To avoid clashing with Mariah, Emery stopped getting up early for coffee and worked longer hours, often getting home after she was asleep. Their communication became limited to a few words on the phone, perfunctory and without emotion.

Running helped relieve Mariah's stress, until one night she tripped and twisted her ankle. Emery was supposed to be working late again, and Mariah limped two miles home. When she opened the door to their apartment, the lights were on. Emery, trying to make up for their last fight, came home early and bought flowers.

His face fell when he saw her limp past him with a swollen ankle. "What happened to you?" He brought ice and an Ace bandage to her chair.

Mariah tired and in pain, spoke without thinking. "I tripped and sprained my ankle about two miles from here. What do you care? Why didn't you tell me you were coming home early? I could have used some help."

"I'm not the guilty party here. It's not my fault you went running in the dark." Emery backed up and tossed the Ace bandage on the couch. "Wrap your own ankle. I'm going to bed."

Mariah knew she was wrong but wasn't in the mood to apologize. She sat on the couch, wrapping the ice loosely around her ankle, and decided to sleep there for the night. The wonderful life she had worked so hard to achieve felt like it was slipping away.

Chapter Sixteen

The American College of Obstetrics and Gynecology's annual district meeting was being held in Atlanta the first week of November. Mariah was left in charge of OB-GYN at MACH while the rest of the department attended lectures.

Mariah didn't mind covering for everyone, but one of Dr. Kennedy's hysterectomy patients was having complications. She wanted to discuss the patient with her, but she didn't answer Mariah's pages.

Mariah called Evelyn, the OB-GYN clinic clerk. "Has Dr. Kennedy called me back yet?"

"No, Dr. Gordon. I'll call you as soon as she does." Evelyn had been the clerk at MACH's OB-GYN clinic for fifteen years. She liked Mariah and could tell she needed some assistance. "Is there anything I can help you with?"

"No. One of Dr. Kennedy's patients is having fevers after surgery and I wanted to discuss her management."

"Dr. Gottlieb was in surgery this morning. She might be available soon." Evelyn looked at her schedule. "She doesn't have any patients scheduled this afternoon. Why don't you try to catch her before she leaves?"

"You're brilliant!" Mariah hung up the phone and paged Dr. Pat Gottlieb. Pat was finishing her last surgery and was happy to come to the clinic to talk to Mariah.

"How can I help you?" Pat leaned against Mariah's desk and smiled. Her blond-streaked gray hair was short and curly, which gave her a youthful, carefree look that complemented her bright-green eyes. Pat worked part-time as a civilian gynecologist. She had completed her active duty military commitment at MACH two years ago and now worked as a contracted civilian. Her lifestyle was much improved; she practiced gynecology only, no deliveries and no night call.

"I'm caring for one of Dr. Kennedy's patients who had a hysterectomy a week ago. She's still having fevers after five days of antibiotics. I think she might have a blood clot somewhere. What do you think?"

"I agree. You should get a CT scan and start her on heparin. Anything else I can help you with?" Pat's smiled.

"There's a patient that Dr. Samuelson admitted over the weekend with pelvic pain who hasn't improved after a few days of IV narcotics. She has a normal pelvic ultrasound and no sign of infection. A laparoscopy is the next step, but he's at the conference."

Mariah really didn't want to take Dr. Samuelson's patient to the OR without him, but there seemed to be no other option. If Pat concurred, she would feel better about her plan.

"I agree. She needs to be evaluated with laparoscopy. Want me to assist you? I know Ken; he wouldn't mind. You're taking excellent care of his patient."

"Thanks. I'll call the OR and get her added to the schedule ASAP." Mariah picked up the phone.

Pat was refreshingly upbeat. She quickly put everything into perspective with simple phrases like: "Did anyone die? Was any one maimed? You saved that patient's life." Her clear-cut approach to medicine and life was inspiring. Pat became Mariah's mentor.

Chapter Seventeen

It didn't take long for Laura Reynolds to get fired. As research clinical coordinator, her callous, rude comments prompted several patients to resign from their clinical studies. By the second week of October, she was forbidden to speak directly to any patient or scientist. The clinical research director had never experienced such a difficult employee. The last straw came mid-November, when Laura parked in the director's parking space and left her car overnight while she worked at a second job across the street. The research center prohibited moonlighting, and Laura was fired the next day.

Being fired didn't bother Laura. The HPV vaccine research job required too much patient contact and didn't give her access to what she needed. She began moonlighting across the street at Viriogen, a laboratory facility associated with virus production.

Viriogen contracted with the National Cancer Institute to produce a mutation of the HPV subtype 16 virus. HPV 16, one of the most potent subtypes and often associated with cervical cancer, was chosen as the target virus for vaccine production. A vaccine that induced antibodies to HPV 16 could make patients immune to cervical cancer. Viriogen genetically altered the HPV 16 virus into a stronger, more infectious strain, HPV 16+. The vaccine made against this superstrain, produced a more rapid and effective immune response. No human had ever been infected with this virus; its use was confined solely to research and vaccine production. Viriogen stored the HPV 16+ virus in a refrigerator at the back of the lab.

Laura was hired to work nights at Viriogen doing data entry and supervising the cleaning staff. She enjoyed the solitude of night shifts, and the HPV 16+ virus, locked away inside the refrigerator, excited her.

It was time to put her plan in motion and contact Mariah. Laura called Mitchell Army Community Hospital and was connected to the OB-GYN clinic.

"Can I speak to Dr. Gordon please?"

"I'm sorry, but the doctor has been called to labor and delivery. Can I take a message?" Evelyn, the clinic clerk, never put anonymous phone calls directly through to the doctors.

"This is her friend Laura, from San Antonio. Please tell her I would like to talk to her. I'll give you my number..."

Mariah was surprised—and apprehensive—to get Laura's phone message. She hadn't forgotten their last encounter on labor and delivery at BAMC.

Against her better judgment, she dialed Laura's number.

"This is Laura Reynolds. What can I do for you?"

"Hi, Laura. This is Mariah Gordon. You asked me to call you?"

Laura's voice sounded overly congenial. "Yes. I thought I should at least give you a call since I'm living in Atlanta and almost your neighbor. How is Mitchell Army

Community Hospital treating you?"

Surprised by Laura's friendly introduction, Mariah tried to sound upbeat and social. "Pretty good! How do you like Atlanta? Emery works in Atlanta, too. Small world, isn't it?"

"Yes. My friend, Helen DeVaney, works in your clinic. She's a great nurse practitioner, and very convenient if you need an annual exam!" Laura probed further. "I heard that you and Emery moved in together. Aren't you engaged?"

"Yes. Sort of…It's complicated. Adjusting to my work schedule and his new job has been challenging for us." Mariah was saying more than she wanted. She quickly changed the subject. "How's your new job?"

"Good." Laura hesitated and then added, "Maybe we should meet for lunch. I feel like I owe you after what I said on labor and delivery at BAMC. We could find a place near Emery's office. Where does he work now?"

"Emery works for a law firm downtown, Dunkley and Brown. I don't know the address, but he's always talking about the fun restaurants nearby. Let's pick a Saturday after the holidays."

"Good. I'll call you in January." Laura hung up.

Mariah stared at the phone and wondered why Laura was being so nice to her.

A more pressing issue emerged when Dr. Morales stopped in and notified Mariah he was canceling his patients and going to see a specialist again for his kidney stones. Thanksgiving was next week, and he was scheduled to work the four-day holiday weekend. He needed to take narcotics for pain control and asked Mariah to work the four-day weekend for him. Drs. Samuelson and Kennedy had purchased plane tickets for travel over Thanksgiving. She had no choice.

Mariah wasn't sure how she was going to tell Emery. Instead of calling him with the bad news, she decided to wait until this evening. To help his mood, she stopped on her way home from work and bought meatloaf, wine, and some potatoes. Comfort food and a few aviation magazines might do the trick. She put the meatloaf and potatoes in the oven and laid out the magazines on the table; hopefully he wouldn't come home too late. Normally she would go for a run, but her ankle still hurt. She sat in a chair by the window, reading a journal, and waited for him to come home.

Half an hour later, Emery pulled into the parking lot. Mariah jumped up and met him at the door.

"Well, this is a surprise. Why aren't you out running or in bed already?" He sniffed and smiled cautiously. "Do I smell meatloaf?"

Mariah handed him a glass of wine. "Yes, and baked potatoes. How was your day? You're home early tonight."

"My day was good. One of the partners at the firm came in today and made a point of congratulating me for acquiring a big account. My contacts in Philadelphia were crucial to the deal, and he let me know he appreciated my work." Emery sipped his wine and leaned back on the couch. He was handsome in his suit, and his smile was a nice change. "How was your day?"

Mariah replied a little too quickly, "It was good. All my patients are doing well." She frowned as she looked into her wine glass. She felt guilty that all this goodwill was put on because she had to tell him about Thanksgiving. Everything was going so well; she wondered if she should postpone telling him the bad news.

Emery noticed her expression. "Really? Because your face says otherwise. What happened?"

Mariah squirmed. "Nothing happened." She was completely unable to lie and hated to break the good mood with her news. "Dr. Morales's kidney stones are bothering him again."

Discussing Mariah's work cooled Emery's warm smile. "That's too bad. Is he going to get something done about them or just keep taking time off every time they cause pain?"

"I don't know. If he has surgery or lithotripsy, he'll be out on sick leave for up to six weeks. And he still might not be cured." *I need to keep the conversation pleasant*, she thought. "Here are a few magazines I picked up for you. Would you like another glass of wine?" She got up and went to the kitchen to check on dinner.

"Yes." Emery followed her into the kitchen. He wanted to warm the evening up again. Giving her a hug, he said, "Thanks for thinking of me," and kissed her neck. "So what is it you have to tell me?"

"Nothing!" Mariah turned to face him and leaned against the sink. "Well, there is a problem now that Morales is sick again," Mariah continued reluctantly. "I have to work the Thanksgiving holiday weekend."

Frustration spread over Emery's face. "Perfect. We were going to take a vacation together, remember? Why can't someone else work the holiday instead of you?"

"Everyone else had plane tickets and travel plans." Mariah was sorry the instant she spoke.

"We had travel plans, too." Emery took his glass of wine back out to the living room and sat on the couch.

Mariah followed, trying to salvage the evening. "I'm sorry. I should be off for Christmas. We can plan a trip somewhere together and make all the arrangements ahead of time. Where would you like to go? Europe? Paris? Rome?"

Emery rubbed his forehead like he had a headache. "We can't make plans because you can't guarantee you won't have to work." He looked at Mariah and continued, "I'm sorry to say this, but since you'll be busy, you shouldn't mind—I'm still going to Pennsylvania to see my folks for Thanksgiving."

Mariah let out a small sigh, but thought, *At least he's sorry about the situation and isn't angry with me.* "I understand. I hope you have fun, and we can do something special when you get back," Mariah said solemnly and hugged Emery. "Let's eat. I'm starved and the potatoes smell delicious."

"That's the meatloaf that smells so good. Why

don't you have some?" Emery teased.

The discussion and compromise brought them closer together. Laughter and lively conversation accompanied dinner, and later they made love with rekindled passion.

Chapter Eighteen

The alarm clock interrupted the deep sleep that follows a night of true passion. Emery enjoyed a quick cup of coffee with Mariah at the kitchen table before going their separate ways. Emery had an early conference in Atlanta, and today was Mariah's OR day, which began promptly at 7:00 a.m. She had two surgery cases and an afternoon meeting with the hospital commander to present her safety plan.

Mariah's presentation was perfectly timed. Earlier that month, the Institute of Medicine (IOM) had published a landmark national report entitled "To Err is Human." Their research established that medical errors caused almost one hundred thousand preventable deaths every year in US hospitals across the country. The article cited medication errors and poor communication as leading contributors to the fatalities.

Mariah was anxious to begin addressing safety issues at MACH under the auspices of the IOM's report. The ectopic pregnancy diagnosed but untreated for three days still haunted her. Family practice residents delivered babies on labor and delivery with varying amounts of supervision. Doctors, required to work two or three nights on call in a row due to staffing shortages, denied any effect of fatigue on their decision-making and surgical skills. Dr. Morales had felt her patient safety plan was compelling but controversial, and didn't want to be involved. He suggested Mariah brief the hospital commander herself.

Colonel Riley was board certified in internal medicine but rarely saw patients. His clinical experience, however, was invaluable. He understood the intricacies of delivering excellent patient care in addition to the necessities of managing a hospital. At forty-two, Dr. Riley was young for a commander, but his energy and enthusiasm inspired his staff and department chiefs. Mariah hoped the IOM's report would encourage the commander to recognize that MACH, like all hospitals, was vulnerable to medical errors that harmed patients.

Hurrying down the administration wing's hall, Mariah nearly ran into a master sergeant as she turned the corner to enter the commander's office. Colonel Riley's secretary, Mrs. Phyllis Trainor, looked up over her reading glasses with disapproval as Mariah skidded to a halt in front of her desk, three minutes late.

Mariah smiled. "I'm Dr. Gordon, and I have an appointment with the commander."

"Yes, and you're late. He just took a phone call. Have a seat." Mrs. Trainor motioned to a straight-backed chair next to the closed door. It was like the detention chair in her middle school.

Mariah sat down, crossed her legs, and checked her uniform for glove powder and scuffs. Her white lab coat was clean, though not pressed. With just a few minutes to gather her thoughts, she rehearsed her safety plan presentation: *Patient safety is every doctor's highest concern. Poor communication is the main cause of medical errors. Teamwork is superior to hierarchy for improving   safety   and   communication.   Improving communication skills and teamwork is the premise for my patient safety plan.*

Colonel Riley opened his office door. "Hello, Mariah. How are you?"

He was younger and taller than Mariah remembered. "Fine, thank you. I mean, 'fine, sir.'" *Damn, I never get that "sir" right. Now I sound like an idiot.* "Thank you for seeing me, sir."

"You're welcome. Come in and have a seat." He smiled and stepped aside so Mariah could enter his office, winking at Mrs. Trainor's scowl.

"Mrs. Trainor noted on my schedule that you want to discuss a patient safety plan for labor and delivery. I was not aware that it was unsafe on labor and delivery."

Mariah launched into her presentation. "It is safe on labor and delivery, but that's not good enough. I'm sure you agree that as doctors and administrators, we can never become complacent about safety, especially in high-risk areas of the hospital like labor and delivery and the OR. My patient safety plan is designed to ensure safe practices are always front of mind and practiced by all members of the health care team." Mariah took a breath and continued.

"The Institute of Medicine's report 'To Err is Human' should be a wake-up call to us all. Like the rest of the country's hospitals, Mitchell Army Community Hospital is not immune to medical mistakes. My plan uses a team-focused approach, similar to CRM, developed by the aviation industry."

"I'm not familiar with CRM. Can you explain what you mean?" Colonel Riley looked skeptical and picked up a pencil so he could doodle while Mariah continued.

"CRM stands for crew resource management. It is an aviation management strategy that empowers everyone in the cockpit with the responsibility for safety while flying the plane. Maintaining situation awareness, pointing out problems, and communicating are duties shared by all members of the team when crew resource management is employed."

"And how would this help us on labor and delivery?" He looked up from his doodle.

Mariah sensed she was losing the commander's attention and made her pitch more relevant to MACH. "Remember the stat C-section Tuesday night last week? It was done under local anesthesia because the OR was busy with an appendectomy. If the OR and labor and delivery teams were aligned, they would have communicated their situations and known about the laboring patient before starting the appendectomy. Removing hierarchy and replacing it with a team-focused approach and encouraging communication among all team members is the platform for my patient safety plan."

"You want the doctors, who are ultimately responsible for the patient's care, to give up their standing in the health care team?" Colonel Riley tapped his pencil doubtfully.

"No sir, I want them to be the leaders of the health

care team. They should listen to input from the team and acknowledge that, although they know a lot, together the team knows more. Just like the pilot from United Airlines Flight 232 that successfully crash-landed in Sioux City, Iowa, said, 'If I hadn't used CRM, if we hadn't listened to everybody's input, it's a cinch we wouldn't have made it,'" Mariah finished and waited.

Colonel Riley put his pencil down and asked, "Do you have your plan written down so I can read it?"

Mariah placed a four-page summary on his desk. "What do you think? Are you supportive?"

"Your idea is compelling. Let me get back to you after the holidays." He took her report and shook hands, indicating their meeting was over.

Mariah walked past Mrs. Trainor's desk and out into the hallway, disappointed with the commander's reaction. *Was that a gigantic waste of time?* She felt deflated, and her enthusiasm fizzled.

Thanksgiving was a long, lonely holiday for Mariah. Emery returned Sunday night; Mariah came home exhausted on Monday afternoon. Tuesday morning, the alarm clock woke them up before 6:00 a.m.

Emery pulled the pillow over his head and complained, "Why do you have to get up so early? It seems like you just got home."

Mariah answered from the bathroom, "You know Tuesdays are my OR days. My first case starts at seven."

Emery resented the fact that Mariah's career always came first. He began swearing under his breath every time her pager went off. Emery's family didn't help matters. Mariah knew they didn't approve of his relationship with her. She suspected visiting his parents over Thanksgiving fueled his frustration. Mariah stopped calling from the hospital to say she was leaving to come home.

Two weeks later, while hurrying down the back stairs in an effort to get home early, Mariah passed Jeremy Strong going up to labor and delivery. Jeremy was a certified registered nurse anesthetist and new to Mitchell Army Community Hospital. Mariah had met him briefly in the OR a few days prior. He was tall, blond, and in very good shape, with a deep voice that made her think of a country music singer.

He paused for a moment as Mariah raced by. "Hey, Mariah! I'm on my way to do that epidural on your labor patient."

"Thanks, Jeremy, but I have to go. I signed that patient out to Dr. Kennedy. Are you on call tonight?"

"No. They're so backed up with cases in the OR, I thought I'd help out and get this epidural done for Casey."

Mariah was impressed. "Wow, that's nice of you!" Since being late was Mariah's primary concern, she couldn't help but ask, "Your wife won't mind you being late?"

"I'm not married." Jeremy started to climb the stairs again. He turned back to Mariah and added, "My girlfriend and I broke up a few months ago."

"Well, good luck with the epidural. The patient is a little 'fluffy.'"

"Fluffy?"

Mariah was trying to be gracious. "Yes, um...she is short for her weight. You know what I mean."

"Oh! Thanks for the heads up." He laughed.

"Have a good night." Mariah turned and kept going down the stairs.

What a nice guy, she thought as she went out to the car. Once in the driver's seat and out on the highway, she called Emery.

"Hello." He sounded tired.

Mariah tried to cheer him up. "I'm on my way home. Want me to get anything? Ice cream?"

"No, just come home. It's almost eight o'clock." He sighed.

Mariah gripped the steering wheel. This relationship felt like it was imploding, and she wasn't sure what to do.

Chapter Nineteen

A week before Christmas, Mariah sat watching the fetal monitor on labor and delivery. The tracing was ambiguous. Subtle changes in the baseline heart rate and variability were worrisome, but not significant enough to warrant intervention. Fetal heart rate tracings were often like this, and Mariah never completely relaxed until the baby was safely delivered.

As she stared at the monitor and signed off charts, she felt hands touch her shoulders and begin massaging the knots of tension away. This felt much too comforting to be happening at work. A small sigh escaped her lips before she turned to find Jeremy playing masseur.

He pulled a chair up and sat next to her. "Anything I can do to help around here?" He and Mariah were friends, but a few nurses' eyebrows were raised at Jeremy's intimate gesture.

Instantly feeling embarrassed, Mariah looked around awkwardly and suggested, "There are several nurses here in need of massages. Who's next?" She stood up to put some distance between her and Jeremy.

Mariah wasn't sure where this friendship was going. She liked Jeremy; he was fun, always in a good mood, and made her laugh when she was stressed. He understood what life was like in the hospital. He even shared the same frustrations and fears involved with taking care of complex patients in the OR and on labor and delivery.

Mariah stole a second to compare him to Emery, who was always suspicious and second-guessing her feelings. He was often unhappy and frustrated about the small amount of time they spent together. Where was the bright, witty guy with the funny grin? She knew he was commuting to Atlanta each day so they could live together.

All she wanted was a happy relationship and a successful career as a doctor. How did everything get so hard? Was there a future for their relationship?

Right now, Mariah decided she didn't care. She wanted a break from labor and delivery and suggested ice cream from the dining hall. As she and Jeremy walked away, one of the nurses answered the phone, then turned and asked, "Is Mariah still here? Her boyfriend, Emery, is on the phone."

"No," said Maybel. "Mariah just left. Take a message."

At home later that night, Mariah was in the shower, and the phone rang. Emery answered and spoke a few words, asked a question, and hung up. As Mariah emerged from the shower, he was waiting, holding her towel.

"Thanks." She smiled and wrapped herself up after toweling off her hair. Emery kept looking at her.

"What's up?" she asked.

"Who is Jeremy? And why is he calling you at home at nine o'clock?" Emery turned and walked out of the bathroom, obviously angry.

Mariah knew sooner or later this might happen. She put on her bathrobe and followed Emery out to the living room where he was sitting in the recliner, stewing. They sat in silence, and Mariah tried to understand Emery's feelings. He was jealous of all the time she spent away from him, and he was jealous of her friendship with Jeremy.

"Jeremy is just a friend from work. I don't know why he called. He knows I'm living with my boyfriend."

"Fiancé," Emery corrected, though they had not talked about getting married in months.

Mariah countered, "Are you jealous of Jeremy? Because that's ridiculous,"

Emery returned, "Being jealous would imply that I care enough."

Mariah knew Emery was jealous of the time demands made by her medical career. "You don't mean that." But it was getting to a point where she needed to decide if this was what she wanted in a relationship. She picked up her towel and went to bed.

Christmas was a few days later, and Mariah took the whole week off. They planned a quiet Christmas morning together in their apartment. Mariah decorated a little tree and bought Emery a nice watch, which she wrapped and put under the tree. She was happy to see another small package next to hers on Christmas morning

They had not really talked since the night Jeremy called. Mariah had wanted to get past all that before this morning, but the right moment never occurred. They drank coffee quietly at the kitchen table and stared at the little tree.

Mariah started, "I'm sorry about the other night," and reached out to touch Emery's hand.

Emery smiled and kissed her hand. "I'm sorry, too."

Mariah got up and handed Emery his gift. "Let's not fight anymore and have a nice Christmas together."

Emery handed Mariah the little package. "I agree, and Merry Christmas."

They smiled awkwardly as they opened their gifts. Emery seemed pleased with his watch, and Mariah pointed out it was engraved: "Yours forever. Love, Mariah."

Mariah was shocked to find an antique diamond ring inside her gift box.

"That's my great-grandmother's engagement ring. I want you to have it as your engagement ring." Emery slipped it on Mariah's finger; it fit perfectly. "I had it sized from the college graduation ring you never wear."

She got up and hugged Emery "It's beautiful! I hope your parents don't mind. I love it. Thank you." She hoped this would somehow put an end to all their disagreements.

Emery added, "My parents loved the idea. We planned everything over Thanksgiving."

The week passed in harmony with reading, talking, and revitalizing their relationship. Y2K arrived with surprisingly little disruption, and they hoped that was a good omen.

Chapter Twenty

Laura stood at the research lab's hood and pipetted 10 cc of HPV 16+ virus from a refrigerated storage vial into a small plastic test tube. She pushed a rubber stopper securely into the top of the tube. It was early, and the lab was deserted. Yet Laura moved quickly and replaced the unused portion of HPV 16+ into the lab's refrigerator and locked it. She put the test tube filled with orange viral liquid in her lab coat pocket and glanced around the lab. No one observed or suspected anything.

Posing as Mariah, Laura had called MACH's OB-GYN clinic over a month ago, confirming the date and time of Mariah's annual exam. Her appointment with Helen DeVaney was today at 1:00 p.m.

Back at her desk, Laura carefully grasped the stoppered test tube in her pocket. Alarmed to feel moisture on the outside of the test tube, Laura quickly inspected the cap to make sure it wasn't leaking. Condensation from the cold liquid made it feel wet. She wrapped a paper towel around the test tube and placed it in a pocket of her purse.

Before leaving the lab, Laura placed a phone call to the OB-GYN clinic at MACH. "Hello. I want to speak to Helen DeVaney. My name is Laura. Yes, I'll hold."

Laura hated to call the clinic again, but she had no choice. Helen didn't have her own extension. While on hold, Laura sat down at her desk and started sifting through the papers.

"Hello. This is Sergeant Oaks in charge of the OB-GYN clinic. I understand you are looking for our nurse practitioner, Major Helen DeVaney? She's not scheduled to be in the clinic until this afternoon. Is there something I can help you with?"

"No." Laura hung up quickly and pulled her day planner out from under a pile of unopened mail.

Laura found Helen's home phone number scribbled in her calendar on January 5, the day she had called her to set up lunch.

Helen DeVaney was an old acquaintance who had worked at MACH for the past three years in the OB-GYN department. Laura met Helen in 1993 at the Army Nursing Corps' Officer Basic Leadership Course. Helen was a nurse practitioner from Texas, recently divorced, and hoping to start a new life.

Laura had used the Army Nursing Corps scholarship to fund her graduate nurse practitioner degree, and signed a four-year army active duty commitment. Unlike their youthful Army Nursing Corps comrades, Helen and Laura were both thirty years old, and each had extensive postgraduate training. With so much in common, they gravitated together during the Nursing Corps' training.

"Hi, Helen. It's Laura. I just wanted to confirm where we're meeting for lunch."

"Yes, I thought we'd meet at the Japanese steak house right off the highway at the Fort Benning exit. I'm scheduled to see patients in the afternoon, so let's meet at eleven thirty. That will give me time to get back to the office before one o'clock."

"See you then." Laura hung up the phone and walked out to her car. The chilly January air was perfect to ensure the virus remained active for several hours.

Helen was surprised to hear from Laura two weeks ago. They had not spoken or corresponded in years. Helen remembered meeting Laura at the leadership course and couldn't remember why they had drifted apart.

Chatting about old times at lunch with Laura reminded Helen why she let their friendship fade. Their jobs were all they had in common. Conversation was forced and centered primarily on Helen's job at MACH's OB-GYN clinic. As they were splitting the lunch bill, Laura asked Helen for a tour of her office.

Helen forced a smile. "Sure. You can follow me. In case we get separated, just turn right at the karaoke bar, and you'll see signs for Fort Benning. Follow the signs for the hospital, the clinic is the low, gray building on the left."

Once in Helen's office, Laura picked up her afternoon schedule. "Twelve annuals this afternoon?"

Helen sighed, "Yes. And if I don't give each and every patient my happy, caring face, I'll hear about it from the commander's office. I received two 'nasty-grams' last week because patients claimed that I rushed them and didn't seem interested in their problems."

Laura reviewed the list of names, adding absently, "Isn't it enough that you provide good care for your patients? Do you have to *care* about them, too?"

Helen smiled and then stood up. "Before I start my clinic, I need to 'powder my nose' in the ladies' room." Pointing to her clinic schedule, Helen added, "I think you know my first patient, Dr. Mariah Gordon. Didn't she take care of your sister before the car accident?"

"Yes. I recommended you to her. Take good care of her for me." Laura smiled.

Helen left for the restroom. "Of course."

Alone in Helen's office, Laura reached down and found the test tube in her purse. Helen's exam room was adjacent to her office, and Laura quickly slipped inside. She went to the exam table and pulled out the top drawer between the stirrups; two metal speculums lay on a pad inside. Laura realized Helen's medical assistant needed to restock this drawer before the afternoon started, and time was short. She discarded one speculum, sprinkled the viral solution over the other, and closed the drawer. Back in the office, she settled into her chair again.

Helen returned a moment later.

"That's better. Now where is Mariah? I hope she isn't going to be late."

Laura stood up. "I must get going. I'll let you know when I'm in Columbus again. Send me the dates of your conference in Atlanta." She picked up her purse and walked into the hall.

Mariah almost collided with her.

"Hello, Laura." Mariah stiffened. "How are you?"

"Fine." Laura forced a smile, remembering she had called Mariah a few months ago and needed to act friendly. "You look as if the Georgia heat and humidity agree with you."

Mariah smiled coolly, "Nice seeing you," and hurried into Helen's office.

As Laura walked down the hall, she passed Sally, Helen's medical assistant, entering Helen's exam room. She pushed a cart full of supplies for the busy afternoon: slides, paper gowns, and more metal speculums.

Sally arranged the speculums in size order with all the handles facing to the right. Since there was only one speculum in the drawer, Sally added ten more and carefully placed them all in order. As she pushed the drawer closed, she noticed moisture on her gloves. *Were the speculums wet?* Sally wondered. She knew these speculums were washed, sterilized in an autoclave, and then stored unwrapped until she restocked the exam table. They were never wet before.

Mariah's pager beeped as Helen completed her medical history. She pulled her pager out of her lab coat pocket to see who was paging her. "Dr. Brown is covering labor and delivery so I can get my exam done. Have you met him yet?"

Helen smiled. "I met him yesterday in the clinic. He seems bright and very cute."

Mariah looked at the numbers displayed on her pager. "Yes he is. And it's wonderful to have another doctor to share night call, especially since Dr. Kennedy will be leaving soon. The ER is paging me. Do you mind if I call them back?"

"Go right ahead. You can use my phone and then go into the exam room to get undressed. I'll start my next patient in another office." Helen pushed her phone over to Mariah and got up to leave. "Let me know if you have to leave, we can always reschedule your exam for another time."

"OK. But I really want to get this exam over with today." Mariah smiled so sweetly that Helen realized it was a joke and chuckled as she walked out of her office. Mariah dialed the ER number from her pager.

"This is Dr. Gordon."

"Please hold for the PA..." The ER clerk put Mariah on hold while she called the physician assistant to the phone.

"Hi, Dr. Gordon. This is Howard Blake. Your patient, Rose Bouton, just showed up in our ER, and she doesn't look good."

Mariah wondered what Howard meant by "not looking good." She asked, "What's wrong with her?" Mariah realized that she'd never heard from David about Rose's cervical cancer evaluation. She'd assumed Rose had the surgery and was recuperating.

"The family states she couldn't have any more surgery or radiation because her cancer had spread throughout her body. She was sent home with pain medication and a consult for hospice. She's here today because her pain is no longer controlled with morphine pills. She's also vomiting and looks very dehydrated. I was going to call internal medicine, but they said you were her doctor."

Mariah felt defeated by Rose's advancing cancer. "I'll be happy to admit her and consult internal medicine myself. Can you order some blood work and put her on a morphine drip for me?"

"Sure, when will you be down to see her? Her family is very anxious."

Mariah looked at her watch. "How about thirty minutes?"

"Sounds good. What floor do you want her admitted to?"

"The GYN floor." Mariah put the phone down and went into the exam room.

Mariah was disappointed. Rose was going to die. Medicine could not cure Rose and was only marginally able to relieve her pain.

Mariah quickly undressed and sat on the exam table. She shivered in the thin paper gown as the air conditioner blew a cold draft over her back and shoulders.

Helen opened the door a few minutes later. As she began the exam, Mariah's beeper went off again. Helen fished it out of Mariah's pocket in her jumbled pile of clothes. Mariah reached for the beeper and saw the dreaded stars of light arranged into the characters, "Labor and delivery stat."

"I have to go." Mariah jumped off the exam table and began putting on her clothes.

"OK. We'll reschedule later." Helen didn't mind performing one less exam that afternoon.

Mariah dressed quickly and ran out the door in less than a minute.

Sally entered the exam room, wiped down all the surfaces, and pulled clean paper over the exam table. She noticed that the Pap smear slide she had labeled "Gordon" had not been used and the speculums were untouched. She threw the unused slide away and set up for the next patient's exam and Pap smear.

Chapter Twenty-One

Mariah arrived to find labor and delivery in chaos. The delivery room door was wide open; Jeremy and an OR team were busy setting up for an operation. Mariah saw Dr. Terry Brown standing at the end of the delivery table holding something; the patient looked unconscious.

The labor nurse explained, "The patient delivered her baby, and then her uterus inverted and delivered with the placenta still attached. Dr. Brown tried to replace the whole thing, but it wouldn't go back inside her!"

Uterine inversion is an obstetric emergency where the inside of the womb follows the baby and delivers through the vagina. The patient often gets light-headed or passes out due to tension on her internal organs. The key to managing the situation successfully is to immediately replace the uterus. The longer it takes to get the uterus back inside the pelvis, the more serious the situation becomes. From the looks of this situation, it was already serious.

Mariah stepped around an OR nurse and asked Dr. Brown, "What can I do to help?"

"Scrub now. If I can't replace her uterus soon, we'll have to open her up."

Mariah nodded and as she surveyed the situation asked, "Why don't you remove the placenta?"

"It'll bleed too much." He was trying to compress the mass of tissue and push it into the pelvis through the birth canal.

Mariah replied, "What have you got to lose?" Her eyes motioned to the OR crew; Jeremy gave her a thumbs-up. "We can support you if there's heavy bleeding, and we can do a surgery if it doesn't work."

Dr. Brown looked around the room and agreed. "OK." Then he announced to everyone in the delivery room, "Everyone stand by, I'm going to detach the placenta." He pulled the placenta off the uterus. The bleeding was profuse, but he quickly pushed the uterus back into the pelvis. He called to Jeremy, "Give her 20 units of Pitocin and an amp of Methergine IM." Within seconds the patient responded.

Dr. Brown looked relieved. "Thanks, Mariah."

Mariah took off her gown and gloves and smiled. "I didn't do anything." She left the crowded delivery room but waited at the nurses' station before going to the ER.

As Jeremy left the delivery room, Mariah caught his attention. "Hey, Jeremy."

"Hi, Mariah. Haven't seen you in a few weeks. Your boyfriend sounded pretty mad when I called that night. I just wanted to ask you a question about a patient." Jeremy flashed her an innocent smile and sat down to write a note in the patient's chart.

"He's doesn't like other guys calling me." Mariah felt awkward having this conversation on labor and delivery, but wanted to get it over with. "Can we still be friends?"

Jeremy didn't look up until he finished his note.

"Fine with me." Tossing the chart onto the desk, he added, "See you later," and walked away.

Mariah wondered why he acted so hurt. Was every man's ego fragile? The phone on labor and delivery rang as Mariah started to leave. The clerk called her back, "Dr. Gordon! There's a phone call for you."

Mariah was impatient; she needed to see Rose in the ER. "This is Dr. Gordon."

"Hold for Colonel Riley." Mrs. Trainor placed Mariah on hold.

Mariah let out an exasperated sigh until the commander's phone engaged. "Hi, Mariah. I wanted to let you know that I read your patient safety plan, and I discussed it with Dr. Slater, the chief of surgery. You know Bob Slater, don't you? He has some concerns and wants to meet with you before we go any further. Can you set that up?"

Mariah rolled her eyes, thinking, *As if I don't have enough to do.*

"Sure, I'll call Bob and set up a meeting. Thanks, Colonel Riley."

The ER was busy as usual. Rose's chart was filed in the GYN/Room Three slot next to the ER nurses' station. Mariah scanned her labs and vitals. Thankfully, everything looked pretty normal, and except for some mild dehydration, pain was Rose's primary problem.

Mariah smiled as she entered room three, although Rose looked terrible. "Hi, Rose." Her family was clustered around her bedside. "I heard you didn't have surgery at

Walter Reed."

"No. Dr. Mettson said the cancer had spread to my lungs. He offered me chemotherapy, but I refused. Hospice is all I have left." Rose looked down at her swollen legs. "The pain is horrible, and they put a tube in my bladder because I couldn't pee. I started vomiting yesterday, and now I can't keep anything down. Can you help me?" She looked sad and desperate.

"Yes. I'll make you comfortable right away. After a day or two of IV fluids and nausea medication, you should be able to go home on IV morphine for your pain." Mariah pulled out her stethoscope.

Rose sighed, leaned her head back on the pillow, and almost smiled. "Thank you for taking care of me."

While completing Rose's admission paperwork, Mariah thought, *Why do the nicest patients always develop a terminal illness?*

She went to her office and tried calling Dr. Slater. She dialed the surgery clinic and asked to be put through to his office.

"This is Dr. Slater."

Mariah went straight to the point. "Hi, Bob. This is Mariah Gordon. The commander asked me to call you about my patient safety plan."

"Hi, Mariah. He briefed me about your plan and I think it has some good ideas. I wanted to talk to you about how the plan was going to go over with some of the surgeons. You know we like to be 'captain of the ship' and we don't take kindly to having our authority challenged."

Bob was joking but wanted Mariah to understand that her plan might be unpopular with his surgeons.

Mariah expected this response. "I understand. I'm not asking them to give up any authority. I want them to effectively lead the health care team that is caring for their patient. It's like being a quarterback on a football team instead of a professional golfer. The 'game' of providing health care is not just about the doctors, it's about the whole team including the patient and the patient's family." Mariah knew this was too much to convey over the phone. "Let's meet and discuss it face-to-face."

"OK. I get what you're saying. Can I bring a few surgeons to our meeting?" He suggested, "Next Monday at seven? We can meet in the conference room before Morning Report."

"Sounds good. See you then." Mariah hung up and looked at the chart on her desk. Her first patient was Captain Roberta Stevens, the patient she had operated on for a ruptured ectopic pregnancy her first day at MACH. She was here for her annual checkup.

Chapter Twenty-Two

The winter had been hard on Mariah, Emery, and their relationship. They agreed a long weekend together was in order. The Gulf of Mexico was an easy five-hour drive and perfect for a getaway weekend. Pat Gottlieb recommended a cute hotel on the beach near Destin, Florida.

As they drove across the Georgia state line into Florida, a cold front blew in from the gulf bringing gusts of wind and rain. Water collected on the highway, making the driving difficult.

While Emery concentrated on the road, Mariah sat quietly, absorbed in her own thoughts. Their busy work schedules made it easy to sidestep any meaningful conversations about the status of their relationship. Three months had passed since Jeremy's evening phone call. Mariah was still concerned about the jealous side of Emery she had seen that night. She wore Emery's ring but hadn't made any wedding plans. She needed reassurance that Emery was right for her.

The little hotel on the beach looked desolate in the storm. Rather than unpack in the rain, they left their bags in the trunk and found a cozy restaurant nearby to wait out the bad weather. Betsy's Bistro had an impressive wine list, offered steak for Emery, and had a salad bar for Mariah. Free from distractions, they snuggled together in a booth and listened to the rain and wind outside.

Mariah scrutinized Emery as she sipped her wine. He was smiling and telling funny stories about colleagues at work. She had forgotten how well they fit together; his shoulder was the perfect height for her head to rest upon. It was uncanny how often Emery voiced Mariah's thoughts or began a sentence that she was about to start. All her misgivings melted away and she was convinced that Emery was her perfect match.

"Emery, do you know how much I love you?" Mariah boldly voiced the words that were filling her mind.

"Whoa! That's a heavy phrase coming from you, Mariah." Emery took another sip of his wine. "I love you too, hon. We've been through a rough winter, and I want us to reconnect. I must admit, though, it's hard for me to play second fiddle to your career. Let's not forget that I have an important career, too." His face was serious. "Let's just focus on enjoying the weekend together."

Mariah, put off by his reply, decided not to comment on her feelings any further. "I'm ready for dessert. How about you?"

"Sure. Call the waitress over and order whatever you want." Emery checked his watch. It was eight o'clock, and the storm was raging just as strongly as when they had arrived a few hours ago. "Let's check the weather when we get back to the room. This storm sounds like it's getting stronger."

Hand in hand, they ran through the downpour to the car. The local weather station covered the storm like it was big news. Four years ago, Hurricane Opal hit

Pensacola so hard that buildings and small businesses along the beach were wiped out without a trace. The population rebuilt, but the tension rekindled whenever a storm blew in from the Gulf of Mexico. The news showed a yellow-green band with red areas spreading across the entire Florida panhandle. "It looks like we're in for a wet weekend." Emery turned the TV off and joined Mariah in bed.

"Perfect." She snuggled against him and turned off the light.

Away from the pressures of careers and everyday living, they found the love that brought them together. The stormy weather made the hotel room cozy, and they enjoyed hours in each other's arms, making love, laughing, and just being themselves. It was like the old days in medical school.

For Mariah, the weekend reaffirmed her relationship with Emery. She felt they were kindred spirits, meant to live their lives together. Looking at him with his blue eyes, happy smile, and large hand holding hers, she could see years ahead and imagined their wonderful, happy life together.

Chapter Twenty-Three

As April turned into May, Evelyn brought bunches of magnolia blossoms to work, and the lemony scent filled the clinic. Dr. Kennedy departed, and a feeling of rebirth permeated the OB-GYN department. Mariah was happy again.

One Wednesday afternoon, Helen pulled Mariah aside in the hallway of the clinic. "Have you ever seen a patient with persistent yeast and pelvic pain? I swear, I have six patients who keep calling me with similar problems; I tried yeast creams, but nothing works. Am I missing something?"

"Not sure. I'm happy to see one or two, if you like," Mariah offered.

"Thanks. I'll have Evelyn schedule a few for you next week." Helen looked relieved to have a plan.

The next day, two patients, now complaining of pain and bleeding, were seated in the waiting room, and Mariah pulled Helen aside. "Two of your patients are in my walk-in clinic today. Both are complaining of bleeding now."

Helen assured Mariah, "They weren't bleeding before."

Tammy Perkins was twenty-three years old. She'd had deep pelvic pain for the past month. All Helen could find wrong was a slight yeast infection. Tammy woke up this morning with a lot of pain and bleeding and came to the GYN walk-in clinic.

Mariah reviewed Tammy's chart. Helen had seen her for an annual exam four months ago—everything was normal, including her Pap smear results.

Mariah entered the exam room holding the chart. "Hi, Ms. Perkins. What brings you to the walk-in clinic?"

"I've been having pelvic pain for weeks and this morning I started bleeding really bad. I'm scared."

Mariah was confident she could diagnose the problem. "Don't worry, we'll find out what's wrong."

Mariah's exam showed a bleeding mass covering Tammy's cervix. On closer inspection, there were bubbly polyps protruding from the mass. "Your cervix is the problem. It looks abnormal, and I should take a biopsy or two."

The biopsies caused brisk bleeding from Tammy's cervix. Mariah applied pressure and a cautery agent, but the bleeding intensified. Despite her best efforts, the blood overflowed onto the floor, splashing Mariah's clogs. Mariah threw a towel down on the floor to absorb the blood and continued holding pressure against the diseased cervix.

"Tammy, your cervix is really bleeding a lot." Mariah motioned to Sally, her medical assistant, to open the vaginal packing material. "I'm going to have to pack your vagina with gauze."

While Mariah pushed the gauze tightly against the cervix, Sally wiped up the blood. By the time Tammy sat up, all signs of bleeding were gone.

"I want to keep you in the hospital for observation until I'm sure your bleeding stops."

Tammy didn't want to stay in the hospital and started to cry. She called her father, an active duty master sergeant.

Tammy's father demanded to speak to Mariah. "Dr. Gordon, This is Master Sergeant Perkins and I have three questions for you: why does my 'little girl' needed to be admitted to the hospital, why can't you stop this bleeding, and what's wrong with her?"

Mariah groaned inwardly as she calmly answered his questions.

Helen's second patient, Stephanie Ashton, was also bleeding. She waited in the GYN exam room with her two-year-old daughter, who explored every cabinet and drawer she could open.

"I'm sorry. I couldn't get a babysitter this morning and my bleeding was so heavy that I was afraid to wait any longer."

Stephanie held her daughter's hand while Mariah examined her and tried to hide any bleeding from the child. Stephanie's cervix was a bleeding mass of tissue just like Tammy's. Before Mariah did another biopsy, she asked Sally to get more gauze and packing to control bleeding.

Stephanie's biopsy didn't bleed as much as Tammy's. Mariah sent her home with strict instructions for rest. Results wouldn't be available until after the weekend. Although she suspected cervical cancer, Mariah was careful not to mention any diagnosis until the pathology results confirmed her suspicion.

Helen approached Mariah at the end of the day. "Thanks for taking care of my patients. I heard Tammy stopped bleeding and you sent her home."

"Yes. Can't imagine anything except cervical cancer that could cause those lesions. How could they grow so fast? They both had normal Pap smears within the last year." Mariah got onto the elevator and pushed the button for the fifth floor; she was on call.

What bothered Mariah the most was that these women had very aggressive-appearing tumors, yet no risk factors for cervical cancer.

Labor and delivery was busy, and Mariah worked her way through the night and Friday morning.

Recalling the romantic weekend in Destin made her smile as she drove home. Sadly, all the warmth and tenderness from that weekend quickly evaporated into their workday routines; Mariah found it difficult to be affectionate after a long day of work. Hoping to re-create the loving atmosphere, she stopped to get a bottle of wine on the way home.

"How was your day?" Mariah greeted Emery at the door with a smile and a glass of wine. She was rested after a nap, and dinner was ready; the apartment smelled delicious.

"Long." Emery pecked her on the cheek and dropped his briefcase on the nearby chair. He took the wine glass from her hand and, taking a big swig, walked toward the bathroom.

Mariah picked up the briefcase and put it next to the desk. She sat at the kitchen table and waited for Emery to reappear. "What do you want to do this weekend?" she asked when he walked back into the kitchen.

Emery opened the refrigerator and refilled his glass of wine. "I'm scheduled to fly Saturday and Sunday. The weather has been so rotten lately; I'm hoping to log a bunch of hours in the cockpit."

Mariah's face fell. "I'm off all weekend. Can't you reschedule so we can spend time together?"

Emery sat down and sipped his wine, staring at her. "Why do I have to reschedule my weekend because you're free? My life counts in this relationship too. We can plan to do something after I go flying."

Mariah was deflated; her enthusiasm for the weekend disappeared. "Sure. Let's do something when you're done flying." She picked up her wine glass and went to the kitchen to serve dinner.

Later that night, she tried calling Jenna, her best friend from residency. Married over ten years to her high school sweetheart, she must have some advice about relationships. Their answering machine took her message.

Emery walked into the bedroom smiling, but Mariah picked a fight just to feel something besides lonely and empty. The next morning Mariah pretended to sleep while Emery left for the airfield.

She was in a bad mood, and exercising didn't help. Mariah hoped running some errands would change her outlook.

While picking up dry cleaning, Mariah ran into Colonel Riley. "Hi, Colonel Riley, sir." Mariah wasn't sure what to call him outside of the army post.

"Hello, Mariah! Please call me Norman. Why aren't you doing something fun and enjoying this beautiful day?" Norman folded his uniform over his arm and smiled, acting like he had time to chat.

Happy to see a familiar face, Mariah tried to be funny. "What's more fun than going to the dry cleaners?"

Norman chuckled. "You need to get out more."

Mariah smiled at the irony and agreed. "You're right." Doing errands was the last thing she wanted to do that day.

Norman heard her disappointment. "Try to have a good day. See you later."

Mariah regretted appearing so obviously unhappy. "I will, sir. Thanks."

"Please, call me Norman." He turned to leave.

"Thanks, Norman."

On Monday morning, as Mariah was leaving for work, Emery announced, "I'm going to DC for a few days. There's a conference the partners want me to attend. I should be home Thursday night. Want me to get you anything?"

Mariah shook her head. "No, thanks. Have fun." She filled her travel mug and blew him a kiss good-bye.

The chief of pathology called Mariah that morning as she entered her office. "Hello Dr. Gordon. I'm calling you because the cervical biopsies you sent us from Tammy Perkins and Stephanie Ashton both show invasive cervical cancer. It appears to be aggressive and undifferentiated. I can't tell you more until I have more tissue. Are you planning to do a cone biopsy?"

Mariah sat down. "Yes." The reality of two cervical cancer diagnoses in these young healthy women was staggering. "Thanks for calling me."

Before treating cervical cancer, an evaluation is performed to determine how far the cancer has spread. This is called "staging." How far the cancer has spread will determine which treatment is most effective. Tammy and Stephanie each needed a CT scan to look for cancer in their urinary system, lungs, and bones. The evaluation also required a trip to the operating room to look for spreading cancer inside the bladder, rectum, and uterus, and a cone biopsy of the cervix. The pathologist studies the cone biopsy very carefully, looking at approximately two hundred or more slides for microscopic evidence of cervical cancer invading the tissues. Mariah's initial exam indicated these patients were likely stage 1B, and good candidates for radical hysterectomy — a procedure performed exclusively by GYN oncologists.

Baffled by these unusual cases, Mariah called her old mentor, Dr. David Mettson, at Walter Reed.

David reassured Mariah. "I hear your concern and agree these sound like abnormally aggressive tumors. Send the patients up to Walter Reed once you complete their staging, and we will take care of them."

Mariah hung up and picked up her schedule. Two more women with bleeding and pain were scheduled to see her.

Chapter Twenty-Four

In June, Dr. Morales's kidney problems worsened, and he was reassigned to an administrative position without clinical duties. Dr. Samuelson completed his army commitment and joined a practice in Virginia. Dr. Kennedy had left in March. The OB-GYN department shrank from five doctors to two: Mariah and Dr. Terry Brown.

The commander recognized this problem and tried to enlist help from local, civilian ob-gyns, but there was little interest. The only solution was to buckle down and work hard until "fresh recruits" arrived in August. One hundred deliveries were predicted for each month throughout the summer. Even with Dr. Parsons, the contracted civilian ob-gyn, taking call on Wednesday nights and Saturdays, life for Mariah and Dr. Terry Brown was going to be grim.

Mariah and Emery talked about the summer workload and agreed it would be a good time for Emery to take vacation and visit his family.

The strain of extra call nights and the young women with cervical cancer took its toll on Mariah. She became tired and anxious.

Running alleviated the stress until she tripped again, this time in the hospital parking lot. One of the ER medics saw her fall and helped her back to the ER. They xrayed her foot, diagnosed a sprain, and sent her back to labor and delivery with a walking splint.

Later that evening, an ambulance brought another woman with bleeding to the ER. Mary Beth Flint worked nights as a cocktail waitress. She had been experiencing deep, aching pelvic pain for weeks and started to notice some bleeding. While carrying a tray full of martinis, she grew lightheaded and stumbled. The drinks slid off the tray and spilled as she hit the floor. The bar became silent as everyone watched a puddle of blood form around her, mixing with the spilled martinis. Mary Beth guessed she must have cut herself on broken glass, but the martini glasses weren't broken. The bartender called 911, and the ambulance arrived ten minutes later.

Mary Beth was losing blood fast. Her pulse was rapid, her blood pressure was low, and she looked very pale; she was going into hypovolemic shock. The EMTs started two IVs and ran fluid in "wide open." They inflated military antishock trousers (MAST) around her legs to squeeze blood to her heart and brain, and quickly wheeled Mary Beth to the ambulance.

As Mariah hobbled into the delivery room to deliver a baby, her beeper went off showing the ER extension. She asked Shelly Baker, the labor and delivery nurse in charge that night, to call the ER for her as she backed through the delivery room door. She could tell it was going to be another busy night.

Once the baby delivered, and the mother and newborn were stable, Shelly leaned her head in through the delivery room door and called Mariah over. "The ER needs you to evaluate a patient who is bleeding ASAP."

Mariah quickly hobbled down the back stairs to the ER. She went straight to the clerk's desk to find her patient's chart, but it was not there. Mariah hoped the message was a mistake but Candy, the ER clerk, handed her the chart for trauma room one.

Mary Beth Flint was lying in Trendelenburg position on a board with her legs encased in MAST trousers. Dr. Kline met Mariah in the doorway and filled her in on Mary Beth's status. Every time they tried to deflate the MAST, Mary Beth's blood pressure would drop, so they left them on. The bleeding seemed to be slowing down, but it was hard to evaluate her in this position. Dr. Kline had already called and alerted the blood bank, the OR, the anesthesia doctor, and the surgeon on call.

"Hi, Mary Beth. I'm Dr. Gordon." Mariah bent over Mary Beth's face so she could see and hear her over the commotion in the trauma room. "I hear you lost a lot of blood. We need to do an exam to see why you're bleeding and determine what we need to do to fix it."

Mary Beth nodded.

Mariah tried to perform a brief examination, but the bleeding was too brisk. She tried using two suction devices simultaneously, which removed enough blood for Mariah to see the familiar, distorted, evil-appearing cervix. Mary Beth needed other options than surgery to stop her bleeding. Mariah decided the most prudent plan was to slow the bleeding long enough to transport the patient to the County Medical Center across town.

She called the ER clerk over. "Candy, call the County Medical Center and ask the gynecologist on call if they'll accept a transfer?"

A few minutes later, Candy poked her head inside trauma room one and announced, "Dr. Olvarte accepts your transfer. I told him everything I had from the chart, and he said fine and to send the patient over as soon as you have her stabilized."

"You're a miracle worker!" Mariah called back and pushed packing firmly against the bleeding cervix. "Tell the medic to get the ambulance ready."

Technically, Mariah knew she was transporting an unstable patient, but the alternative was worse. Mary Beth needed the services and expertise of a medical center. Mitchell Army Community Hospital's choices were limited, and Mary Beth could develop DIC, the final downward slide that had cost Penny her life.

Mariah put Mary Beth on the ambulance and, for the first time in her life, said a prayer to help her patient get to the County Medical Center safely.

Chapter Twenty-Five

Mary Beth returned to MACH two weeks later for a postoperative evaluation with her husband, Sergeant Kyle Flint. Although Mary Beth had surgery at a civilian medical center, she was obliged to follow up at MACH for her postoperative care. The large vertical incision on her stomach was draining bloody, foul-smelling fluid. Mariah lifted the dressing off Mary Beth's wound and slowly exhaled.

Mariah looked at Mary Beth. "Your incision is infected, and I must clean that wound in the OR."

Mary Beth sniffed and then started to cry. She had not slept well since the night she was brought to the ER. The County Medical Center stopped her bleeding long enough to diagnose her with microinvasive cervical cancer. The gynecologic oncologist performed a radical hysterectomy, removing her uterus, upper vagina, and one ovary. She was still in pain and felt worse today than the night after her surgery. "I just want to feel better, Dr. Gordon."

Mariah put her arm around Mary Beth's shoulders to comfort her. "You'll feel much better once we treat this infection."

Mary Beth wiped her nose with a tissue, and Mariah quickly finished her examination, paperwork, and consent forms.

Despite broad-spectrum intravenous antibiotics and wound debridement, Mary Beth's infection did not improve. Dr. Brown and the infectious disease specialist agreed Mary Beth needed exploratory surgery to find the source of her persistent infection.

Jeremy helped Mary Beth move onto the operating table. Prior to going under anesthesia, Mary Beth called out, "I love you, Dr. Gordon!"

Mariah replied, "I love you, too, Mary Beth!" But Mary Beth never heard her; she was already unconscious and intubated.

Jeremy taped the endotracheal tube to her cheek, looked over at Mariah, and smiled. "Wow! Can you be *my* doctor?"

Mariah rolled her eyes and began to remove Mary Beth's bandages. The stench of infection stung her eyes, but they were already tearing up. Mary Beth was a young woman like Mariah, and her complications made it difficult for Mariah to remain unemotional.

A pelvic abscess was the culprit, and although Mariah removed the infected tissue, Mary Beth's lungs absorbed the intravenous fluids like a sponge. In order to breathe, she needed a ventilator with pressurized oxygen. Mary Beth went from the OR to the ICU and remained intubated overnight.

The doctor in charge of the ICU approached Mariah the next morning. "Mary Beth is not improving. She's not getting worse, but she is not getting better either. We don't have the resources to care for her if she deteriorates. I recommend we transfer her to an army regional medical center now, while she's stable. I just spoke to the director of Eisenhower Medical Center's Surgical Intensive Care Unit, and they will accept her, but we need to send her ASAP. A fixed-wing aircraft with a ventilator can be dispatched immediately from Fort Gordon and will arrive in two hours."

As if in a trance, Mariah nodded in agreement. She had to inform Mary Beth's husband right away.

Sergeant Flint sat in the corner of the dimly lit ICU waiting room. He looked apprehensive and scared.

A small movement drew Mariah's attention to Kara, Mary Beth's six-month-old baby, sleeping in her carrier. Preoccupied with keeping Mary Beth alive, Mariah forgot she was also a new mother. Mary Beth's life was hanging in the balance, and Mariah needed to act fast to tip the scales in her favor.

She spoke quietly. "Mary Beth is stable, but our ICU specialist feels it's too soon to remove her breathing tube. He also recommends transferring her to Eisenhower Medical Center, where she can get around-the-clock care by specialists. She'll be flown to Fort Gordon in the next few hours." Her voice cracked just a little as she finished.

Sergeant Flint stared at his boots; his shoulders sagged as if the energy he was using to get through this ordeal was draining away. "She's going to die, isn't she?" he whispered.

"No!" Mariah was emphatic. "She's very sick, but Mary Beth is a healthy young woman. She will fight this infection and get well. I'm sure of that,"

Sergeant Flint looked up. "Can I see her?"

Mariah hated to see tears in a soldier's eyes. "Yes. I'll tell the nurse you're coming."

Mariah returned a moment later and held Kara as Sergeant Flint quietly entered the busy ICU. His wife lay unconscious with an endotracheal tube protruding from her mouth. Mariah watched through the glass as Sergeant Flint gently held Mary Beth's hand and looked into her face. A single tear clung to Mary Beth's long eyelashes. While he stared, the tear slipped down her cheek.

He reached out, brushed it away, and quietly cried. "You're gonna be OK, baby. I love you so much. I'll take good care of Kara until you come home." Then he squeezed her hand and walked out of the room.

Kara began fussing in Mariah's arms as he returned. She was hungry and wanted breast milk, not formula. Sergeant Flint sighed as he lifted Kara out of Mariah's arms and placed her into the carrier. She started screaming as he quietly buckled the safety strap and carried her out of the ICU.

Mariah remained seated in the ICU waiting room. Discussing Mary Beth's life-threatening situation followed by holding her baby had a sobering effect. She took advantage of the solitude to reflect on her own life.

Her personal life was built around her being a stoic, hardworking young doctor; her career always came first. In residency, she had prided herself on being like "Teflon," maintaining an emotional protective barrier to prevent the anguish and heartbreak of her patients' illnesses from affecting her. Mariah realized excelling in a single area to the exclusion of others resulted in an unbalanced, unhappy life. Experiencing the beauty and enormity of living could only occur when life was balanced between work, family, and friends.

She needed to make some changes. She wanted to find Emery and tell him face-to-face about her revelation—she could see their future life together, and it was so much more than just her career. It was more than just his career. It was about being happy together and sharing every wonderful moment of everyday life.

Sadly, Mariah couldn't leave the hospital or try to explain her feelings to Emery over the phone. She was on call and overloaded. The internal glow from her epiphany cooled as she admitted three more patients in labor and another woman from the ER with bleeding. The pregnant patients labored all night; two delivered without complication, and one needed a C-section at 4:00 a.m. Mariah admitted the woman with bleeding and planned to take her to the OR in the morning before clinic. The alarm shattered her single hour of sleep. She winced as she pulled herself up and sat wondering how she would get through the day.

Fortunately, coffee and a shower worked their usual magic. Within half an hour, Mariah was her old self again, clicking down the hall to the OR with a smile on her face. She wasn't going to let a hard night of call ruin her revelation. In the OR, she laughed and made jokes with Jeremy. The case went well, and Mariah grabbed another coffee on her way to clinic. She had routine OB clinic; it should've been an easy morning.

Brenda Gibbons awoke that morning with some cramps and a little spotting. She was only twenty weeks pregnant and had an appointment at 8:30 a.m. When the OB clinic receptionist called to move her appointment back to 11:00 a.m. due to Mariah's surgical case, she just said, "OK, I'll come in at eleven."

By the time she arrived at the clinic, she was quite sure she was contracting. As she followed Sally to the exam room, she felt warm water trickle down her right leg.

Brenda told Sally, "I think I might be leaking fluid."

Sally handed Brenda a gown and sheet. "Get undressed and I'll tell Dr. Gordon."

Mariah walked in a few minutes later. "Hi, Brenda. Sally says you think you're leaking fluid. Anything else going on? Any cramping or bleeding?"

"Yes. It started this morning. At first I wasn't sure if I was contracting, and I knew I had this appointment...It's nothing serious, is it?" Brenda started to get scared.

"Not sure. I have to examine you first."

Mariah's exam found that Brenda was about to deliver her fetus in the exam room. Brenda's cramping had dilated her cervix, and the amniotic sac was leaking fluid. Mariah explained to Brenda that she was going to deliver her baby soon—nothing could be done to stop her from delivering, and the baby was too premature to survive. Mariah tried to stay unemotional, but it was hard not to let Brenda's anguish touch her.

Mariah ordered an epidural for Brenda to block any pain from the contractions or delivery. Brenda's mother arrived and demanded to know why her daughter's preterm labor was not stopped, why Brenda's baby was not going to survive, and why Dr. Gordon couldn't do more to fix the problem. Mariah did her best to explain the facts; it was a long afternoon for everyone.

By the end of the day, all the encouraging thoughts and revelations from the prior evening were lost in the morass of her patients' complications. Mary Beth was in the ICU at Eisenhower Medical Center, and Brenda delivered a stillborn fetus.

She was getting ready to leave when her phone rang. "This is Dr. Gordon."

"Hello, Mariah. How are you?"

Shocked to hear Laura's voice, Mariah tried to keep her answer brief. "Terrible." But once started, Mariah couldn't resist unloading her emotional day. "My patient just lost her twenty-week fetus, and HPV is ruining my life."

Laura paused before asking, "What do you mean?"

"There have been at least ten cases of young women with cervical cancer. One patient is on a ventilator at Eisenhower Medical Center and might die of complications from her radical hysterectomy. And we're short staffed and working every other night until August." Mariah didn't mean to open up so fast, but it had been a long day.

"How's your health? I assume you're taking care of yourself."

"I'm fine. Helen did my annual, and everything was normal." Mariah, remembering that afternoon, reminded herself softly, "I never did get that exam."

Laura sounded surprised. "You didn't?"

Mariah didn't mean for Laura to hear her comment, and now had to explain. "No. I was called away to an emergency on labor and delivery." *Why was Laura asking about her annual exam?*

Laura had heard enough. "I have to run." She hung up and slowly picked up an empty test tube lying on a counter in the lab.

Her phone rang again.

"Hello..." Laura smiled. "Hi, Emery. Thanks for calling me back. It was fun bumping into you this morning at the coffee shop. I was just going out for a drink and dinner and wondered if you wanted to join me." Laura persisted before Emery could decline her invitation. "I'm pretty sure Mariah's on call tonight. It must be hard to work late and commute two hours when your partner isn't even home half the time." Laura paused. "OK. I'll see you there at seven."

She hung up the phone. Laura remembered their relationship in high school. She was sure she could fill the void Mariah's career created in their relationship.

Then she looked up Helen's home phone number and left her a message.

Chapter Twenty-Six

It was getting dark when Mariah parked her car. She was exhausted, but still excited to share her revelations with Emery. The apartment was dark he wasn't home yet. She opened the door and clicked on the light. The answering machine blinked with a message.

Emery's voice sounded cheerful. "Hi, hon. I knew you'd be tired after being on call, so I'm going out with some friends. Don't wait up I'll be late. Bye." The message ended with a click.

Disappointment smothered the last shimmer of inspiration.

Mariah opened the refrigerator but nothing appealed so she crawled into bed, still wearing her uniform, and cried herself to sleep.

Several hours later, Emery crept into their bedroom. He smelled like wine and perfume. Mariah woke up, but pretended to be asleep as he got into bed. Once asleep again, she dreamed of seeing Emery with another woman at a restaurant. In her dream, Emery refused to acknowledge her and laughed as she stood sobbing before him.

Mariah awoke in the morning sad, drained, and depressed. Emery smiled and made coffee, but she couldn't talk to him. Feeling exhausted and dejected, Mariah left for work without saying good-bye. She needed an easy day at work. Fortunately, her clinic was not overbooked, and all the patients were straightforward. She even had time to go to the dining hall for lunch.

Jeremy was just sitting down at a table as Mariah paid for her lunch. Mariah approached his table with her lunch tray. "Is this seat taken?" she asked.

Jeremy smiled and pulled out the empty chair next to him. "Howdy, stranger! Did they let you out for good behavior or are you a fugitive from the OB-GYN clinic?"

Mariah placed her tray next to Jeremy's. "Both. If I'm not back in thirty minutes, they'll send the dogs after me."

It felt good to joke after last night's turmoil. Eating and laughing together made the time fly, and Mariah smiled all the way back to the clinic.

Afternoon clinic was busy until the ER called. Dr. Brown was on call for the ER, but Rose Bouton, Mariah's private patient, was back and in terrible pain again. She was dying.

The sight of Rose sitting on the exam table made Mariah pause in the doorway Rose looked like a skeleton. Cancer had consumed this once-robust, enthusiastic woman. Her thin, gaunt face was drawn tight in pain. Rose's sister and husband sat next to her, looking sad and tired. Rose's cancer caused such agony that she cried out at night and no one slept. Emily was absent.

Mariah ordered a morphine drip and admitted Rose to the GYN floor. The medication brought prompt pain relief. Rose smiled for a few minutes and then fell asleep. Her sister went home to do the same, and Hank dozed in the chair next to her bed.

Mariah noticed the bag draining Rose's bladder never accumulated any urine. She ordered a blood test to check Rose's kidney function. She suspected Rose was in kidney failure and hoped she would slip into a coma soon; uremia was a merciful way to die.

Ob-gyns rarely provided care for dying patients. Oncology specialists and internal medicine doctors were trained to care for the terminally ill. Mariah, however, felt a duty to keep Rose as her patient. She traded call with Dr. Brown so she could care for Rose through her final night.

At 1:00 a.m., Mariah was called to evaluate Rose's pain control. The room was dark, and although Rose was deeply sedated, she still moaned occasionally. Her husband sat next to her the IV pump's faint blue light illuminated his haggard face. He held onto Rose's pale hand firmly.

Mariah felt awkward interrupting their silent intimacy as she stepped up to the machine. "I have to manually override the IV pump settings to allow Rose to have more morphine,"

Once programmed, the machine beeped loudly, shattering the silence.

"How's she doing?" Hank asked as he gently placed Rose's hand on the hospital bedsheet and rubbed his eyes.

"I don't think she has much longer." Mariah clicked the machine's panel shut, and it whirred as a new bolus of morphine was pushed down the tubing to Rose's arm.

He nodded and lowered his head as Mariah left the room.

At 4:00 a.m., Mariah was called to pronounce Rose dead. Hank stood by her bed and looked lost. Mariah gave him a hug, and the night nurse began to gently ask about plans for Rose's funeral. Mariah grabbed some Kleenex and busied herself with paperwork until she regained her composure.

Desolate, Mariah walked the dark halls of the hospital. It was too early to be awake, too late to go sleep and she shivered in her scrubs. The extreme hour of the day allowed her mind freedom to consider thoughts that waking hours would censor. Mariah decided she'd had enough of medicine.

I wish I could talk to someone.

For a moment, Mariah considered calling Emery or even Jeremy. Then she remembered Pat Gottlieb would be in the clinic later this morning. Pat would help with her problems.

Pat greeted Mariah as she entered her office, "Good morning, Mariah. Looks like you were on call last night."

Mariah followed Pat into her office. "Yes, I was on call, and I can't do this anymore. The cervical cancer cases are making me emotional. My patients are dying. I'm on call every other night, and when I do get home, Emery's not there. I need help."

Pat put her briefcase down and sat behind her desk, sipping coffee from her travel mug. "I was wondering when you were going to ask for help, but I didn't expect you to give up. You don't strike me as a quitter."

"I'm not a quitter. I just think I made the wrong choice."

Pat cupped her mug in her hands. "Do you really want to give up your career? All the time and effort you spent preparing yourself to be a doctor?"

Mariah sat down. "What good is any of it if I'm unhappy? All I ever wanted was to be respected by my colleagues and patients, and loved by someone in a special, personal relationship. Now I am so overworked that I don't care what my patients or colleagues think, and my relationship is on the rocks." Mariah stood up and leaned over Pat's desk, speaking more softly. "I feel like a failure at everything. I hate to admit it, but I give up. No more!" Mariah started waving her arms like an umpire calling a runner out at home plate. "Finis! Adios! Adieu!"

"You're getting a little dramatic…"

Mariah sat down and composed herself. "I do that when I'm tired and emotional."

Pat began calmly, "Is there no other way out of this? Can we get your patient load decreased? Have you looked at these cervical cancer patients' charts? Is there anything the patients have in common?" Pausing for a moment, she offered, "Why don't you give me a list of all their names, and I'll look it over with a fresh pair of eyes?

There are just too many cases for this to be an isolated increase in cervical cancer. And on a different note, can we rework your schedule so you have less pressure and a little more free time?"

"Don't know." Needing to fully unload her troubles, Mariah changed the topic from work to Emery. "Emery's cheating." Mariah started to cry.

Pat grabbed a handful of Kleenex, handed them to Mariah, and continued, "Let's look at this situation clinically." She began her usual questioning. "Has anyone died? Well, yes, but Rose was already sick with terminal cancer when you met her. Has anyone been maimed? Well, yes, the HPV patients have been losing their uteruses."

Pat's approach wasn't working, and encouraging Mariah wasn't easy. "Let's try looking on the bright side. Even if Emery is fading out of the picture, I'm sure that you're still loved by your mother."

Mariah rolled her eyes in reply.

Pat gave up trying to help Mariah emotionally. "You came to me seeking help, and I will make sure that we relieve your work burden, but you'll have to manage your personal relationships."

Mariah nodded, and even though very little was actually done, she felt better. She picked up a pen and wrote down the names of the all the women who were affected with cervical cancer in the past few months, she knew them all by heart.

Chapter Twenty-Seven

A week later, Laura pipetted another 10 cc of HPV 16+ virus into a plastic test tube and pushed a rubber stopper into the top of the tube. Laura had found out Mariah's Pap smear appointment was today, and she was convinced this time her plan would work. She planned to surprise Helen at MACH and plant the virus before Mariah's examination.

Trying to be discreet, Laura removed her gloves and placed the test tube in her lab coat pocket. As she opened the refrigerator to replace the vial of HPV 16+, Laura noticed her pocket was wet. Reaching inside her pocket to investigate, she discovered some of the viral liquid had leaked out of the test tube and moistened the back of her right hand. Laura quickly pushed the stopper further down into the test tube and removed her dampened lab coat as she replaced the HPV 16+ vial in the refrigerator. Realizing her hand was contaminated Laura immediately went to the sink and began scrubbing both her hands with a bleach solution.

The HPV 16+ was potent. The lab technicians were warned to avoid any skin contact. Knowing what it had done to Mariah's patients, Laura was concerned about her exposure. She used bleach to clean the outside of her test tube and placed it carefully in her purse.

Mariah walked into the dining hall for lunch and was surprised to see Laura Reynolds sitting with Helen. Uninterested in making small talk, Mariah tried to sneak out with her lunch tray.

Helen called, "Hi, Mariah!" Her eyes were pleading for rescue. "Won't you join us?"

Mariah placed her tray next to Laura's and noticed a red rash on her hand. "What happened to your hand? Is that a burn?"

Laura put her hand in her lap, out of view. "Yes. That's what I get for trying to cook." Smoothly changing the subject, she asked, "Any improvements in your work schedule?"

"We're still really short staffed. I'm not enjoying my job very much." Mariah couldn't help complaining.

Laura was a master at making someone who already felt bad feel worse. "You're surprised about being overworked? Did you forget that you *chose* this specialty?" Back in her groove, she added, "How's Emery? Or have you found someone else?"

Mariah sighed and ignored Laura's question about Emery. Laura was right; she chose this field. She shouldn't be surprised at the workload. Maybe she should stop complaining so much.

"The hardest issues for me are the cervical cancer cases. I've never referred so many young women for radical hysterectomy; it's heartbreaking. These women have little kids or wanted to have kids. It makes me want to stop working and have my kids now, just in case something like that happens to me." Mariah stopped. Helen and Laura were both staring at her.

Laura broke the silence. "You shouldn't act too fast. Aren't replacements graduating from residency soon?"

Mariah admitted, "We get two new OB-GYN grads in six weeks. I just hope I can last till then."

Laura became impatient and snapped, "Of course you can." All of a sudden she was in a hurry to leave. "I'd love to stay and chat with you girls, but I have to get back to Atlanta." Laura quickly picked up her tray and purse, and left.

As she walked away, Mariah shoved Helen's shoulder playfully. "Lunch again with Laura! I didn't realize you two were such good friends!"

"We aren't. She showed up in my office this morning saying she was in the area and invited herself to lunch with me." Helen picked up her tray and then turned to Mariah. "Didn't I see your name on my clinic schedule this afternoon? Are we finally going to do your Pap smear?"

Mariah had forgotten all about her appointment. "I made that appointment months ago. There's no way I have time for a Pap today. I have to get back to clinic."

Helen sat back down at the table. "No problem. Now I have time to enjoy another cup of coffee." She picked up her coffee mug and filled it at the self-serve coffee urn as Mariah got up to leave.

Mariah passed Colonel Riley in the hall as she left the dining hall.

"Good afternoon, Colonel Riley." Mariah smiled as she walked by.

Colonel Riley replied, "Hi, Mariah. I saw your name on my schedule this afternoon." Mariah looked surprised, and he continued, "We're following up on your patient safety plan."

I can't believe I forgot two appointments today!

"Of course!" Mariah hated appearing disorganized. "I've been a little busy lately."

She hurried back to her office and checked her day planner. There it was. "Meet with Col. Riley @ PSP at 4:00 p.m." Her clinic schedule was blocked too.

Mariah was surprised to see that her appointment with Helen was also blocked off. *I really need a secretary to keep me organized. Maybe I can still get that Pap over with.*

Sally was carrying a bucket full of speculums as Mariah approached Helen's office. "Dr. Gordon, these speculums are all wet again. I'm going to get new ones before your exam. Do you mind waiting a few minutes?" Sally asked.

"No. My schedule was blocked for thirty minutes. Is Helen back from lunch yet?"

Helen walked toward them as they were talking. "Here I am! How long has it been since we started this exam? Six months?" Helen smiled. "If you still have time and Sally can get things cleaned up, we can finally do your Pap smear."

Sally pushed by them with her bucket muttering, "I know it was six months ago because that's the first time the speculums were wet. Have to change everything in that drawer."

Mariah and Helen both wondered what Sally was talking about.

The exam only took five minutes, and Mariah used the extra free time to review all the paperwork for her patient safety plan. With Bob Slater's help, she had convinced the surgeons her plan would improve patient care without undermining their authority. She was excited to start training, but not before the new doctors arrived.

The afternoon clinic was busy, and Mariah started to get a headache.

She walked out to the GYN clinic's front desk and pleaded, "Evelyn, I need coffee and chocolate! Can you help?"

Evelyn smiled. "There's a fresh pot of coffee in the break room, and I have an emergency bag of chocolate." She opened the bottom drawer of her desk, and behind her purse was a package of miniature Hershey bars. "Help yourself!"

"Thank you so much." Mariah grabbed three candy bars and went to the break room for a cup of coffee.

At 3:45 p.m., Mariah packed up her patient safety plan paperwork and walked across the hospital to the commander's office. Mrs. Trainor was at her desk, like a bulldog guarding Colonel Riley's door. She motioned to Mariah. "Colonel Riley will see you. Please let yourself in."

The commander was reviewing a chart as she entered. He promptly stood up to shake Mariah's hand.

"Hello, Mariah. I'm glad you found time for our appointment. I know how short staffed you are, and I appreciate all the extra work you and Dr. Brown have done to keep the department running smoothly. The administration continues to get glowing reports from your patients, too."

Colonel Riley took off his reading glasses and motioned for Mariah to sit in the chair across from his desk. "Before we talk about the patient safety plan, I want you to know that I just hired a locum tenens ob-gyn for July and August. I'm sorry it took so long. Your specialty is in demand everywhere."

Elated, Mariah started asking, "When will the doctor arrive? What kind of experience does he or she have?" She could hardly control herself. "Thanks so much, Colonel Riley!"

"Please, call me Norman. Here's Dr. Sutherland's file; it looks good. He trained at Madigan Hospital and then worked in Landstuhl, Germany, where he finished his army obligation. He worked for ten years at a large practice in Washington State before choosing to practice locum tenens."

Mariah quickly looked through Dr. Sutherland's file. "Hmmm, I wonder why he left private practice."

Satisfied, she closed the file and handed it back to Norman. "It doesn't matter. He's coming soon, and that's wonderful! Thanks again, Col—I mean, Norman."

Norman waved it back. "You keep it. I'm putting you in charge of orienting Dr. Sutherland to the hospital. If you have any questions, Mrs. Trainor will help you."

Norman leaned forward in his seat slightly and folded his hands on his desk. "Dr. Slater tells me you made great progress getting your plan approved by the surgeons. I'm impressed; that couldn't have been easy."

Unaccustomed to recognition, Mariah enjoyed explaining her success. "It wasn't easy, but I think the surgeons understand that the increasing complexity of practicing medicine requires a team approach. I want to call the patient safety plan, 'PSP.'"

Norman was impressed. "You're very dedicated. In light of the current OB staffing shortage, I think we should involve nursing and plan for training in the fall. Why don't I put you in touch with Major Nancy Milton, chief of nursing? She does a lot of training and skills assessment. Having her involved will get buy-in from the nurses." He picked up a perfectly sharpened pencil and made himself a note.

It must be nice to have a secretary to sharpen your pencils, schedule your meetings, make your calls, and bring you coffee, Mariah thought to herself and said, "I look forward to working with Major Milton, sir."

Norman stood up and extended his hand. "It's always nice to see you, Mariah. Good luck with Dr. Sutherland."

Mariah shook his hand firmly and smiled. "Thanks again for everything, Norman."

She practically skipped back to her office. Clinic was over, the lights were all off, and Mariah was free to leave. She was so happy, she practically ran to her car. Quickly removing the dishtowels, she turned the radio up and sang along all the way home.

Emery had arrived a few minutes ahead of her and was getting out of his car as Mariah parked Irving. He was talking on the phone and ignored her as he grabbed his briefcase, pushed the car door closed with his hip, and walked toward the apartment building. Mariah parked her car as he disappeared inside.

Mariah cornered Emery in the kitchen, forcing him to end the phone conversation.

Annoyed, Emery said, "I'll have to call you back later." He closed his cell phone and fixed Mariah with a glare. "What's so important that you need to interrupt my conversation with a client?"

Mariah noticed Emery's familiar frown. Over the past few weeks, he had seemed distant and frequently unhappy. "We need to talk about us."

"Really? Why now? Does this moment suit you? Well, it doesn't suit me. There are two people in this relationship, and I count, too. I just got home. I was on a phone call with a client the whole drive home. I want to sit down, have a beer, and collect my thoughts. You can't just hit me with 'We need to talk about us' when I walk into the house. Why don't you start over with something more social like, 'How was your day?'" Emery pulled a beer out of the refrigerator.

Mariah obeyed. "How was your day?"

Emery took a long drink of his beer. "Lousy."

Since he didn't ask about her day, Mariah decided to get to the point. "A few weeks ago I asked for help at work."

"Really. I'm amazed. What did they say?" Emery's sarcasm illustrated how far apart he'd grown from her in the past few weeks.

Mariah's enthusiasm for the conversation began to wane. "A locum tenens doctor is coming soon to help us out." Emery did not respond, and she continued, "And, just like I asked for help at work, I wanted to ask for help from you, too."

"What do you want help with?" Emery folded his arms, indicating he no longer really cared.

Mariah suddenly felt like crying. "I want us to be together, to need each other, not to just coexist. I want you to know how much I love you and that I'm sorry that I've been so distracted and distant." Observing Emery's posture, she added, "I hope it's not too late."

"It *is* too late. I'm tired of being last on your list of priorities. Our relationship is a casualty of your career. I was going to tell you this tonight anyway; I rented an apartment in Atlanta. Besides decreasing my daily commute, it will give me some space and let me decide if there's a relationship worth salvaging."

Mariah stood silently, aghast.

She wondered who was really on the other end of the phone when Emery hung up moments ago. "Are you seeing someone else?"

"Aren't you?" Emery's words did not cut her nearly as deep as the look he shot her.

He walked into the bedroom, pulled his suitcase out from under the bed, and started packing. Mariah watched all this like she was witnessing a robbery occurring on a surveillance camera; she was helpless to stop him. She wanted to pull his clothes out of the suitcase and jump inside herself. She tried taking some of his shirts out, but he just flashed her an angry glare, snatched the clothes out of her hands, and threw them back inside the suitcase. He was definitely leaving her.

"Who are you seeing?" Mariah ran after him down the hallway and out to his car. "Who is she?"

Emery turned to her as he opened his trunk. "What difference does it make?" Placing his suitcase inside, he added a phrase he'd obviously been rehearsing. "You get what you give, and now you can make do with what you got." He slammed the trunk closed.

Then he paused and smiled. For a second, Mariah thought the whole thing might be an awful joke. But his face twisted in an evil grin. "Why don't you call Jeremy and see if he's free for dinner tonight?" Laughing, he got in his car and drove away.

Mariah stared at the back of his car. It turned down the street and disappeared around the corner.

"Emery!" she called out, knowing it was too late. "Emery!"

The parking lot was silent. Mariah sank onto the curb and waited, hoping he would come back. After a few minutes, she realized he wasn't coming back and began to cry.

Mrs. Fallon, a neighbor she barely knew, saw Emery leave and came outside. "Are you OK?" She sat next to Mariah and patted her back. "Were you together long? My George left me after twenty years of marriage. I know how you feel. Let's go inside and get you a glass of water." Mrs. Fallon guided her up the stairs to her apartment door.

Mariah felt a little embarrassed at being so emotional. "Thank you, Mrs. Fallon. I appreciate your help. I'll be OK now."

"We all go through hard times, dear. Just knock on my door if you need anything." Mrs. Fallon smiled and turned toward her own door.

"I will. Thanks again." Mariah closed the door.

Inside, the apartment was quiet. And empty. Mariah tried to understand what just happened. Her suspicions were correct; Emery was seeing someone else.

Chapter Twenty-Eight

Distracted by thoughts of Emery with another woman, Mariah found it hard to pay attention at work. She looked up from the chart she was holding and realized she hadn't heard a word her patient had said. "Can you please repeat what you said about your pain?" Concentrating on her patients' problems was nearly impossible.

Mariah's brain would lapse into images of Emery sitting at dinner, candlelight reflecting in his beautiful eyes, holding someone else's hand.

She tried calling Emery's office, but his secretary wouldn't put her calls through to him. She knew he was taking calls from the other woman. How could this be happening? Who was she?

Desperate to know whom Emery was seeing, Mariah tried calling Emery's office and posing as his mother. "Is Emery available? This is Loretta Davison, his mother."

It worked, and Emery's secretary was quite helpful when she wasn't speaking to Mariah. "I'm sorry, Loretta, but Emery is out with a client. Shall I tell him you called?"

"No, thank you, I'll try him again at home but he goes out every night! I know you can't give out private information, but I'm his mother...I just wondered...Is he dating anyone new yet?"

"I shouldn't say anything, but there is a girl named Laura. She called him a few times this week, and they went to lunch together on Tuesday."

"Really? Laura? Not Laura Townsend from his high school, I hope!" Mariah pressed for more info.

"No, I believe her name is Laura Reynolds."

Mariah barely suppressed a gasp.

"Thank you. It's been nice chatting with you. Have a good day." Mariah hung up the phone. Emery was seeing Laura!

Mariah had shut herself in her office to make the phone call, and now her nurse was knocking insistently on her door. Her brain was racing; she wanted drive to Atlanta and confront Emery. After a moment, reality restrained her emotions. She knew she couldn't leave work, and Emery wouldn't see her anyway. Mariah needed to tell someone who would understand how she felt.

She called Jeremy in the OR. "Hi, Jeremy, it's Mariah. Are you free for lunch? OK, see you then."

In the dining hall, Jeremy took a bite from his hamburger and fixed her with a carefree grin. "What's up?"

Mariah suddenly felt embarrassed about her situation. She wasn't sure she should confide in Jeremy.

Jeremy touched her hand. "What happened?"

Mariah couldn't resist his kindness and opened up. "Emery moved out. He's seeing someone else." She looked away, trying not to cry.

"He's such a turd."

Mariah burst out laughing.

"It's true!" Jeremy ate another bite of hamburger. "You're much better off without him."

Mariah couldn't help but wonder if Jeremy had his own motives for comforting her. She smiled and sipped her coffee; maybe he was right.

Major Nancy Milton called Mariah on labor and delivery later that day. Mariah watched the fetal monitors while she took the phone call. "Hi, Major Milton. Colonel Riley told me you would be calling."

"Hi, Dr. Gordon. The commander showed me your proposal and briefed me about your preliminary work with some of the surgeons. Getting buy-in from the other doctors will be tricky, but the IOM report has created a sense of urgency for this kind of training. If we can win over the doctors and show gains in patient safety, your program will be a success."

Mariah was encouraged by Major Milton's enthusiasm—but that would have to wait. One of the fetal heart rate tracings took a nosedive.

"I have to go. I'll call you back later." Mariah hung up the phone and went to the patient's bedside.

"How are you feeling?" Mariah asked her patient as she walked into the labor room. "Your baby's heart rate just decelerated, but now it's back to normal. I need to do an exam; you might be ready to deliver."

The patient smiled. She had an epidural and felt no pain at all. Twenty minutes later, after an easy delivery, she held her beautiful baby girl.

The next day, instead of going to lunch, Mariah practiced her southern drawl with Bernice from labor and delivery. They borrowed the head nurse's office for privacy.

Bernice had transferred from BAMC and was happy to see Mariah's familiar face. Born and raised in Louisiana, she laughed at Mariah's fake southern accent. "Talk slower, Mariah. Make your 'r' sound softer, and slightly slur the last word of each sentence."

Mariah tried again. "Law, I swear I been too good a girlfriend to be treated like such trash!"

"Don't lay it on too thick, or you won't be believable." Bernice shook her head. "I still can't believe Emery left you for Laura Reynolds. Are you sure you want him back?"

Mariah's eyes flashed as she picked up the phone and dialed Emery's office. "No. But I can't stand the thought of them thinking they're so clever. I want to hurt him like he hurt me."

Bernice whispered, "Good luck!" and quietly closed the door behind her.

Armed with her new southern accent, Mariah was determined to make an appointment with Emery. "Hello, this is Betty Shiner, I work for Senator Miller. Mr. Davison and I met at a convention last month in Washington. He asked me to look him up the next time I was in Atlanta, and I will be traveling there next week. Is he available sometime next Friday?"

"Yes, we can work you in at two o'clock. Shall I send you a confirmation?"

"No confirmation needed. I'll be there at two. Thank you." Mariah hung up the phone.

Success! She would meet Emery at his office and confront him about Laura. Mariah hoped once Emery saw how much she cared, he would change his mind and give her a second chance.

Chapter Twenty-Nine

Pat Gottlieb dialed Mariah's extension. "I need to show you something. Can you come to my office right now? I have to go to the OR in a few minutes."

Mariah hurried into Pat's office. Pat motioned for her to close the door.

She held up a paper summarizing her results. "Every patient that you identified has one thing in common. They all saw Helen for an annual exam on January 19 this year. The patients' symptoms began about three months later, and each patient developed an abnormally aggressive HPV infection. I pulled Helen's schedule for that day, and every one of her afternoon patients is affected, except you." Pat placed the paper on her desk.

Mariah suddenly remembered that afternoon. "I never had my exam! I got a stat page to L&D and left before we did the exam." Slowly, Mariah picked up Pat's summary. "You think Helen had something to do with it? Why would she do that? Were the patients getting infected during the examination?"

Pat looked at her watch. "Don't know, but I'm late for the OR." As she rose to leave she added, "We should talk to Helen and Sally together. I'll be back in two hours."

Mariah rose and followed Pat. "Do you mind if I just ask her now?"

Pat stopped her. "I would be very careful. This could be something the MPs need to handle. I'm not sure you should say anything without someone present as a witness."

Mariah couldn't believe her ears! Helen was a great nurse practitioner who loved her patients and was heartbroken over the cervical cancer cases. Why would she infect her own patients? Mariah couldn't wait for Pat.

Mariah tried to sound nonchalant as she passed Helen in the clinic hallway. "Hey, Helen. Want to get lunch together?"

Helen knew Mariah never invited someone to lunch without a reason. "Sure. What's up?"

Mariah froze for a moment. "Nothing, I just wanted to have lunch with you," she lied. "Maybe Pat Gottlieb can come, too."

Helen was sure something was going on. "OK. Call me when you're ready to go."

The three women sat in the dining hall, eating quietly.

Mariah broke the silence. "Helen, Pat volunteered to review the cervical cancer cases hoping to find a common factor."

"Good! I was hoping we could get some answers. Too many to be explained by random chance." Helen looked at Pat. "What did you find?"

Pat looked from Mariah to Helen. "All the patients were seen by you for an annual on Wednesday afternoon, January 19 of this year. The only woman who did not develop cervical cancer is Mariah, and she states she didn't have an exam that day."

Helen spoke in a hushed voice, "Are you suggesting that I had something to do with these women getting cervical cancer?"

Seeing Helen's concerned expression, Mariah quickly spoke. "We don't think you're to blame. We need to find out what links all these cases together. Right now, the only thing they all have in common is an annual appointment with you on January 19."

Hardly relieved, Helen offered, "I'll go over their charts again and talk to my medical assistant."

That was exactly what Mariah hoped Helen would say. "That sounds like a great idea. You do a little research, and we can all meet together on Monday." Mariah's meeting with Emery was tomorrow afternoon, and she didn't want this new information getting in the way.

Pat wasn't sure letting Helen review the charts was a good idea, but she didn't suspect Helen either. "I can't make it on Monday, but you girls go ahead and discuss your results without me." Pat picked up her tray to leave. "My role as data analyst is complete."

Helen used every free moment between patients to comb through the pile of charts Pat deposited on her desk. She shook her head as she reconfirmed that each woman saw her for a Pap smear on January 19.

In her exam room, Helen opened the drawer holding the speculums. She stared at the shiny, metal, duck-billed devices lined up in order by size, fresh from the autoclave. No longer sterile as they lay open to the air on a clean towel, they were appropriately clean and ready for use as per protocol followed by most GYN providers across the country. How could her exam have transmitted an aggressive HPV to those women? And why only that afternoon? Contamination was the only answer.

The next day Mariah planned to leave from the clinic and drive directly to Emery's office for her appointment. A little before lunch, she changed into a stylish, sage-colored dress and put on some makeup. As she walked out of her office, Evelyn waved from behind the clinic's check-in counter. "Good luck, Dr. Gordon!" Everyone in the clinic was rooting for her.

While driving to Atlanta, Mariah tried to compose a compelling opening statement to Emery but had trouble verbalizing her feelings. She wanted an undeniable argument that would convince Emery to take her back. Emery was accustomed to winning debates in the courtroom. Unable to come up with anything better than, "Emery, I know you're seeing Laura, but I'm way better than her," Mariah knew she was in trouble.

Mariah parked Irving in the parking garage across from the law firm. It was too early to appear for her appointment. A small coffee shop was nestled next to the parking garage, and she sat in a booth facing away from the door in case Emery stopped in. Her lunch had no taste, and the *Atlanta Constitution* newspaper couldn't hold her attention. After half an hour, it was time.

No one recognized Mariah because she had never visited Emery's office. The law firm's secretary greeted her warmly. "Hello, Ms. Shiner. Attorney Davison is running late. Please make yourself comfortable." She guided Mariah into Emery's office.

The stakes were high for this meeting, and Mariah looked stunning.

Five minutes later, Emery walked in and stopped short, surprised to see Mariah in his office. "What are you doing here?" Recovering, he added, "You have to leave. I'm busy and have a meeting with a client." He was staring at her dress.

"I *am* the client who scheduled the meeting with you." Mariah's voice was too high-pitched, and she felt herself getting emotional; maybe Emery should see her cry.

"I have to know, Emery, are we really over? I'm not seeing anyone and was never unfaithful. I want you, Emery. Don't you want me? You said we were meant to be together." Her voice choked.

Emery looked away. He walked behind his desk and sat down, putting the desk between them. The silence was so protracted Mariah rose to leave.

"Don't go yet. I've been thinking about you a lot lately. I know who you are and how you are. Over and over, we tried to salvage our relationship. It always failed."

He continued, "It's too much work to be with you. I used to believe that we were meant to be together but I was wrong." He clasped his hands together, concluding his rebuttal with, "I thought we were kindred spirits; we're not."

Mariah bent slightly at the waist, as if she had been punched in the stomach. She reached out but leaned on the sturdy oak desktop instead. Gathering strength and composure, she looked up.

She glanced around his office and noticed there was no trace of their relationship. No picture or evidence that Mariah ever existed.

Loss and sorrow converged as the weight of Emery's words hit her. Tears began to form in her eyes. If she didn't leave immediately, Emery and his office staff would witness her losing her last shred of dignity.

She wanted to scream, *You are such a jerk for not giving me a second chance*. Instead she lifted her chin, slipped the engagement ring off her finger, and calmly said, "You have obviously made your choice. I know you're seeing Laura Reynolds." As she walked out the door, Mariah couldn't help saying sarcastically, "Good luck with that." Stone-faced and composed, Mariah pushed the down button for the elevator. Seeing it was several floors away, she took the stairs instead. Sixteen floors gave Mariah enough time to squeeze the sadness and sting of Emery's rejection out of her heart. Once inside her car,

Mariah thought she'd start to cry. But instead of crying, she began thinking. It was time to move on.

Emery picked up the phone as soon as Mariah left his office. He dialed a familiar number. "Hi, it's me. Guess who just left my office...Mariah." He listened for minute and then added, "She was pretty upset."

Chapter Thirty

The moment after Laura hung up with Emery, her phone rang again. Thinking it was Emery calling her right back, she answered, "What did you forget to tell me?"

Amanda Reynolds's voice rasped, "Have you gotten even yet?"

Startled, Laura answered without thinking. "Not yet."

"What the hell are you waiting for?"

Laura recovered her composure. "My plan takes time. I stole her boyfriend."

"Your love life is not what's important. I'm looking for revenge." Amanda was agitated and a little drunk.

"I'll let you know when it's done." Laura hung up.

After a minute, she dialed the phone again. "Hello, Emery. It's me again. Maybe I should pay Mariah a visit and smooth things over a little. You wanted to take a day off and pick up your bike from her apartment. You could drop me off at the hospital on Monday and get the bike while I meet with Mariah. I think I owe her that much. OK. See you tonight."

On Monday morning, a small noise made Mariah look up from the chart she was working on to find Helen standing in her office doorway.

Helen held out a small calendar she kept in her purse. "Laura Reynolds and I met for lunch on January 19." She pointed to the date on the calendar. It read, *11:00 a.m.-Lunch with Laura at steak house.* "She came back with me to the clinic after lunch. I think you met her in the hall before she left. Do you think she might know something? Isn't she working on a vaccine project right now?"

Mariah said, "I do remember seeing Laura for a minute before our appointment. She recommended you for my annual." Mariah shut her mouth before she disclosed any more facts.

Helen asked, "Want me to call her and ask if she has any ideas about how so many patients got sick that day?"

Mariah rose from her chair. "No. I don't think you should speak to Laura, at all. I'll call her myself."

Helen shook her head. "OK," she said, and left.

Uncovering the cause of these cervical cancer cases was evolving into a criminal investigation. Mariah needed to inform the hospital's chain of command.

Mariah found Bob Slater, chief of the department of surgery, sitting in his office.

"Hi, Bob. Do you have a minute?" Mariah walked up to his desk.

He put his pen down, took his reading glasses off, and sat back in his chair. "Sure, Mariah. What's up?"

"I have a list of patients I want to show you. This is Helen DeVaney's clinic roster from January 19, and every patient on this list, except me, has developed some form of invasive cervical cancer this year."

Dr. Slater sat forward and put his glasses back on. He motioned for her to give him the list of patients.

"How's that possible? Cervical cancer is a pretty unusual, slow-growing cancer. Takes years to develop into an invasive tumor. Especially in women getting their routine Pap smears."

"Correct. The only explanation is they were infected with a virulent form of HPV virus. I believe the speculums in Helen's exam room were contaminated that day with a potent HPV unlike any HPV virus we've ever experienced. Perhaps a virus made by a research lab." Mariah remained standing in front of his desk. "And I think I know who did it."

Dr. Slater pushed the patient list back toward Mariah like it too was contaminated. "We have to take this to the commander of the hospital."

Together they walked to Colonel Riley's office. Mariah worried about Helen being implicated with Laura. She couldn't imagine Helen was involved.

Waiting outside Norman's office, Mariah went through the whole scenario again in her mind. These were serious allegations, and the patients were seriously ill. Mariah worried that Laura might try something else.

Colonel Riley led them into his office, and Mariah began her story. The atmosphere was tense, but Mariah felt her self-confidence build as she explained how the patients became ill, and how she discovered they all had one appointment in common, and her theory regarding Laura. By the end of her explanation, she felt very proud of her detective skills.

"Who else helped you and knows about this situation?" Norman asked.

Slightly deflated at admitting she had help, Mariah gave credit to Dr. Pat Gottlieb and Helen DeVaney.

Norman wrote the names down on his pad. "How are they related to Laura?"

"Helen met Laura at the Army Nurse Corps Officer Basic Training Course, but I don't think they planned this together. Helen would never knowingly infect her patients. She seemed genuinely upset that the cases originated in her exam room. And Pat Gottlieb has never met Laura Reynolds."

"Helen could still contact Laura. We need to call the MPs. But first, tell me more about your relationship with Laura and what could have motivated her to do this."

Mariah took a deep breath. Recounting the events of Penny's death was still difficult for her. While she spoke, Bob was paged away. Norman sat and listened quietly to the whole story. When Mariah finished, he sat thinking for a few more minutes.

"I'll call the MPs and alert them about this case." He lifted the telephone and asked his receptionist to call the chief of military police, then hung up. "They'll want to interview you, Helen, and Pat. In the meantime, don't discuss this with anyone. This could turn into a very big investigation, and we don't want any information leaking."

"Yes, sir," she said, and rose to leave.

"Just a minute. I want to change the subject, if I may." Colonel Riley motioned for Mariah to sit down again. "I've heard a lot of good things about you as a doctor. You take great care of your patients: admitting a terminally ill woman to your service, ensuring her last hours were comfortable and peaceful, and allowing her family to stay with the doctor they had come to know and trust. I know that you're unhappy with the current work schedule, and I hope Dr. Sutherland can fill the gap. Many things need to be changed in the OB-GYN department, and I appreciate your efforts in developing the patient safety plan."

He continued, "I heard a rumor that you are unhappy and considering leaving MACH. That would be a shame. What would it take to keep you here?"

This conversation was taking a different direction than Mariah had envisioned. As Mariah thought about Colonel Riley's question, she noticed he was very handsome, a few years older than she was, and didn't wear a wedding ring. She would have to do her own "investigation" of his availability later.

"I'm committed to implementing my patient safety plan. I still owe three years of service to the army. I'm not going anywhere soon." Mariah stopped there. It was better to say too little than too much.

"Let's meet over lunch next week," he offered.

"OK...sir," Mariah added, acting unfazed by his invitation.

"Please, call me Norman."

As she left his office, Mariah smiled to herself.

Chapter Thirty-one

Mariah was still thinking about Colonel Riley when she walked into her office. Laura sat smiling behind her desk. Mariah froze. She wanted to accuse Laura, but Colonel Riley had insisted on secrecy.

"What are you doing here, Laura?" Mariah stood in the doorway. Emery's face flashed into her thoughts. "I know you're seeing Emery. How could you break us up?"

Laura's smile broadened into an unattractive sneer. "I wish I could take credit for breaking you and Emery up. You did that all by yourself."

Laura's smug expression made Mariah mad. "Get out of my chair and leave my office. I'm going to call the MPs." Mariah moved toward her desk, trying to act menacing.

Laura leaned back further in the chair and asked, "How are you feeling?"

Astounded by Laura's question, Mariah recognized the HPV was meant for her. All the women who contracted cervical cancer on that day were innocent victims of Laura's plan for revenge. "Were you trying to repay me for Penny's death?" Mariah avoided accusing Laura.

Laura smiled too innocently. "What are you talking about?"

Knowing she was the intended target, Mariah tried another way to draw a confession out of Laura. "I feel fine.

Never better." Her smile matched Laura's. "I don't know what you're trying to accomplish, but you failed."

Mariah stared at Laura's hand resting on her desk. The rash was now a dark-brown, scaly mass, resembling reptile skin. "It looks like you infected yourself along with several other innocent patients."

Incensed, Laura replied, "You're responsible. You let my sister die. You weren't punished. Justice needs to be served. Any collateral damage increases your guilt."

Mariah spoke cautiously, trying not to disclose any more facts about the case. She cursed herself for not asking Norman if the MPs were coming to her clinic today.

"I know you blame me, but once Penny's car hit the guardrail, the events couldn't be changed." Mariah spoke calmly as she picked up the phone to dial the MPs: "Hurting me won't bring your sister or her baby back. And your plan failed, I was not infected with your HPV virus."

The bluntness of this statement hit Laura like a slap in the face. She rose from Mariah's desk chair and pulled a 9 mm pistol out of her purse. "Put the phone down." Laura pointed the gun at Mariah. "You think you can walk away without any penalty?"

Mariah remained silent and backed up against the wall of her office. She tried to move closer to the door, but Laura blocked the doorway.

Trapped, Mariah tried again. "You're worse than I ever was. You permanently harmed women just like

Penny: young, happy, innocent. Put down the gun before this gets out of control."

For a moment Laura looked confused and then spoke to herself in a strange whisper, "I must have revenge." Her hand clenched involuntarily, and the gun went off, sending a round through the wall next to Mariah.

Startled and now desperate, Laura lunged for Mariah, digging the gun into her side. She pushed Mariah ahead of her, down the hall to the crowded clinic waiting room. Realizing Dr. Gordon was a hostage, patients started screaming and ducking under chairs for cover. Mothers shielded their children with their bodies and cried for help.

The shouting became muffled as they pushed through the clinic's doors into the deserted hallway. Mariah sensed Laura's desperation.

MPs, sent to interview Mariah, heard the shot and ran down the hallway as Laura pushed Mariah toward an exit. She put the gun to Mariah's temple and turned to face them. "Leave me alone and let me leave, or I swear I will kill her right here."

All attention was focused on Laura—until Emery appeared at the exit doorway.

Opening the door, he was aghast. "Laura, what are you doing?"

Laura waved the gun at the door. "Turn around and leave, Emery."

Mariah screamed, "Don't shoot him!" And then, without thinking, she pleaded with Laura. "Please don't shoot Emery."

Realizing revenge was finally within her grasp, Laura pulled the trigger and Emery collapsed to the floor.

Mariah screamed. Furious and desperate to help Emery, she stamped her black heel deep into Laura's instep, feeling a crunch.

Laura winced, releasing her grip. Mariah immediately ducked to the floor and started crawling toward Emery as the MPs fired. Gunshots echoed down the hallway, and Laura slid to the floor.

Mariah reached Emery as blood pooled around his body. Laura's bullet had grazed his neck, nicking his carotid artery.

"Emery!" She bent over him and held pressure against his neck. He wasn't breathing. She looked up at the MP standing over her. "Call a code! Someone start chest compressions!"

Stabilizing his neck and airway, Mariah breathed into Emery's mouth. An MP began pumping his chest, and a minute later an ER trauma team took over. The EKG showed ventricular fibrillation, which deteriorated quickly despite several shocks. They moved him to the trauma room in the ER, but after twenty minutes without response or heartbeat, Dr. Kline pronounced Emery dead.

Mariah stood stunned outside the trauma room as the trauma team filed out.

She walked into the silent room; a nurse was removing the endotracheal tube from Emery's mouth. He lay on his back, and the bandage on his neck made his head turn slightly in her direction as if he intended to speak a final word.

"Oh, Emery," was all Mariah could say as she gently closed his beautiful blue eyes. His skin felt cold, and she knew he was gone forever.

Chapter Thirty-Two

A week later, Mariah attended a mandatory one-on-one psychological debriefing session required by the hospital.

The hospital counselor began her interrogation. "Let's take a minute and focus on how you're recovering from the events of last week. Are you sleeping well at night?"

"Yes," Mariah lied. *If you count crying yourself to sleep.*

"Are you having any nightmares? Is your appetite OK?"

"No and yes." More lies. *I can't remember the last meal I actually ate.*

Since she was wearing scrubs, Mariah slipped off her clogs and pulled her knees up into her chair. She was confident that this counselor had nothing to offer her grief process; she just wanted to end the session as quickly as possible.

The counselor changed the focus of her questions. "What do you want out of life, Mariah? Do you have a vision of the future?"

Where did that question come from? Mariah thought for a moment. "I want to be happy, have a loving relationship, and a fulfilling career. I want to help people, but I want to have a life, too."

Mariah continued, "Prior to the incident, I felt lost. I wasn't happy with my life."

The counselor pressed, "Tell me how you feel about your career."

"It's a lot more stressful and time-consuming than I planned. Life after residency was supposed to be easier. It's not, and I'm not sure I want this lifestyle. I feel that medicine has failed me—demanding more than I can give. I'm sure this played a huge role in the breakup of my relationship."

Mariah continued without giving the counselor a chance to reply. "I loved Emery, but I knew our relationship was over before Laura killed him." Cautiously, she added, "Is it too soon to think about moving my life forward without him?"

"I don't think the traumatic event you experienced means you can't pick your life up where you left it. A little time and thought devoted to examining your priorities might be in order." The counselor stood up, indicating their time was up.

"Can we meet again?"

"Yes. Using a diagnosis of PTSD, you're allotted three more sessions."

Mariah got up and walked to the door. "Thanks." she called over her shoulder as she pushed through into the outer office. She had permission to restart her life and wondered where to begin.

Labor and delivery was hopping. Dr. Brown had covered for her during her counseling session. No one had delivered yet, and all the paperwork was done. All that remained was to wait for the women's labors to progress.

Mariah wondered what Colonel Riley was doing at this moment and decided he was probably in a meeting. She picked up the phone and dialed his office anyway.

"Hi, Mrs. Trainor, this is Dr. Gordon. Is Colonel Riley available? He is. Thank you...Hi, Norman, I was going to go to the dining hall and wondered if I could take you up on your offer of lunch this week...Sure, I'll see you then."

Three months later, Mariah parked in MACH's administration parking lot and entered the elevator on the ground floor. It was 0700, and as the new safety officer for MACH, she attended the commander's Morning Report meeting each day. Mariah still practiced medicine, but her duties as an ob-gyn had been reduced once the new staff doctors arrived.

The elevator doors opened on the first floor. Two doctors entered and pushed number five.

"Good morning, Mariah." They both smiled.

"Good morning. A surgeon *and* an anesthesiologist going to labor and delivery together? I hope you're attending a patient safety training session." Mariah smiled, exiting the elevator toward the Morning Report conference room.

THE END

Afterword

Cervical cancer is the second most common cancer among women worldwide. In the United States, cervical cancer is the eighth leading cause of cancer in women, killing approximately four thousand women each year. In contrast, worldwide, two hundred and fifty thousand women die from cervical cancer each year. In developing countries where Pap smears are not routine, cervical cancer is one of the most common causes of cancer death for women.

Like most cancers, it's best to diagnose cervical cancer before it spreads. The early stages of cervical cancer have no symptoms—Pap smears are required for early detection. Access to Pap smear testing is the determining factor for early diagnosis and survival; microscopic invasion is almost completely curable. Cervical cancer that has invaded more than a few millimeters is harder to cure, and survival rates fall as invasion increases.

Two vaccines, Gardisil and Cervarix, are currently available to fight this cancer. The World Health Organization has developed guidelines on prevention and control, including vaccination and screening. By the end of 2012, forty-five countries had introduced HPV vaccination. Most of these are developed countries. Given that the global burden of cervical cancer falls heaviest on developing countries, there is still a great need to introduce the HPV vaccine as part of a national public health strategy.

Mariah's patient safety plan is based on TeamSTEPPS, an evidence-based teamwork system to improve patient safety. Further information is available at **http://teamstepps.ahrq.gov**.

Visit **www.normarosebooks.com** to learn more about the author what happens next to Mariah Gordon.

www.ingramcontent.com/pod-product-compliance
Lightning Source LLC
Chambersburg PA
CBHW051423170626
46809CB00006B/2289